THE GLITTER AND THE GOLD

THE GLITTER AND THE GOLD

Marion Chesney

Chivers Press • G.K. Hall & Co.
Bath, England   Thorndike, Maine USA

This Large Print edition is published by Chivers Press, England, and by G.K. Hall & Co., USA

Published in 1999 in the U.K. by arrangement with Robert Hale Ltd.

Published in 1999 in the U.S. by arrangement with Barbara Lowenstein Associates.

U.K. Hardcover   ISBN 0–7540–3729–0 (Chivers Large Print)
U.K. Softcover   ISBN 0–7540–3730–4 (Camden Large Print)
U.S. Softcover   ISBN 0–7838–8597–0 (Nightingale Series Edition)

The text of this Large Print edition is unabridged.
Other aspects of the book may vary from the original edition.

Set in 16 pt. New Times Roman.

Printed in Great Britain on acid-free paper.

British Library Cataloguing in Publication Data available

Library of Congress Cataloging-in-Publication Data

Chesney, Marion.
    The glitter and the gold / Marion Chesney.
       p.   cm.
    ISBN 0–7838–8597–0 (lg. print : sc : alk. paper)
    1. Large type books.   I. Title.
    [PR6053.H4535G55   1999]
    823'.914—dc21   99–18823

CHAPTER ONE

Miss Fanny Page had come to the conclusion that nothing exciting was ever going to happen to her. It was a year since she had left the seminary in Bath, where she had been very happy. The principal had told her father to remove her as the fees had not been paid for a year.

Returning home, expecting to live on gruel and stale bread, Fanny had discovered, to her surprise, that her feckless parents were still living in a fairly grand way. Her father had countered her complaints about the abrupt termination of her stay at the seminary by saying blithely that she was too old to be educated and that intelligent women were highly unmarriageable.

Her seventeenth birthday had just passed. There seemed to be no plans for her future. Her parents were a bright, frivolous pair in their thirties, seemingly without a care in the world. So she settled down to amusing herself as best as she could. There did not appear to be any young people in the immediate neighborhood whom her parents considered to be suitable companions, and so she passed her long days in reading novels and dreaming of handsome men. She still wore her hair down and was dressed in the gowns she had worn at the seminary, which were becoming increasingly short at the hem and tight at the bust.

Despite her added height, she was only a little over five feet tall, and to her despair did not show any signs of turning into the tall, statuesque lady she longed to be. She had a mass of glossy black curls that rioted down her back, rosy cheeks, an elfin face, and huge, brown, sparkling eyes.

Her home, Delfton Hall, despite its grand name, was a square box of a place in the middle of the Oxfordshire countryside, its harsh red brick walls unrelieved by creepers. There were no flowers in the gardens, only shaggy lawns cropped by sheep.

Then, just as she was returning to the house one day after a long walk in the wintry grounds, she was told her mother wished to see her, a rare summons.

Mrs Page was a small woman with improbably colored fair hair and highly rouged cheeks. She was dressed in the latest fashion of thin muslin, despite the chill of the drawing room.

'Ah, Fanny,' said her mother, 'come here and let me look at you, child. Tch! Tch! Too much color in your cheeks. You should not walk so much in the cold. You will get a *blowsy* look. And that gown! What a fright!'

'If you supply me with some cloth, perhaps I can make a new one,' said Fanny, thinking bitterly of all the times before when she had made such a request—only to have it turned down.

'I wish there was time to send your measurements to London,' said Mrs Page, narrowing her eyes and scrutinizing her daughter. 'Never mind. Miss Clement from the village is coming to alter some of my gowns for you. You must look your very best.'

'And why is that, Ma?'

'I do wish you would call me Mother. Did that seminary teach you no style, no grace? We are having a little turtle supper next week. Squire Deveney and Mrs Deveney are returned from London. We have not seen them this age.'

Fanny frowned. 'If I have it right, you said six months ago that Squire Deveney was a wastrel and a gamester . . . and the Deveneys had not a feather to fly with.'

Mrs Page trilled out a laugh. 'You must be dreaming. I adore the Deveneys. Sound family. Good English stock. You must look your prettiest. As a matter of fact, their son, Sir Charles, is due home quite soon.' She kissed her fingertips. 'Such a delightful young man. Knighted for bravery, too. Fought like a Trojan.'

'Charles Deveney must be . . . let me see—twenty-nine, Ma. *That's* not young.'

'Hark at the child! In the prime of life, my sweet.' Mrs Page put her head on one side and her sharp eyes raked her daughter up and down. 'Must be white muslin, but not too girlish. And your hair!'

'I did want to put it up.'

'Long hair is not the thing. You need one of the new crops, like Caroline Lamb. Mr Tulley will need to do it. I'll send John to fetch him.'

'I do not think our local barber knows anything about fashionable crops.'

'Don't quibble. Be a good child and be guided by me.'

Well, thought Fanny in a dazed way, later that day—after her hair had been shorn and the local dressmaker was picking out some of Mrs Page's very best gowns to alter—you never really knew what was going to happen. She looked at her reflection in the glass. Her hair was surprisingly pretty, now a cap of black glossy curls. Poor Mr Tulley had been so nervous of cutting it that he had dropped the scissors several times. Charles Deveney, now Sir Charles. What would he be like? She could not remember much about him. Yet she knew she had met him a long time ago, when she had been ten. But he had seemed to belong to the world of grownups. She had a vague memory of someone tall and fair. Would he turn out to be the hero of her dreams? The boredom of her days had turned her into an excellent dreamer, and so the picture of Sir Charles, at first hazy, grew in her mind and took shape and form. He would be battle-hardened, a seamed, lined face tanned by the Spanish sun. He would be very tall and strong.

She passed the time pleasantly—once she had made a face and form for him—in writing scripts for Sir Charles. At first he would dismiss her from his mind as being too young, but . . . Ma's little donkey carriage would run away with her and she, Fanny, would ride to the rescue, hair streaming—No. She ruffled her short crop. No more hair to stream. But he would be impressed. He would see the rescue, and the light of admiration would bring warmth to his stern face. They would walk together in the gardens under a full moon and he would look down at her and murmur, 'Your beauty unmans me.' Fanny experienced a qualm. She did not think herself beautiful at all. But a man in love would think her so, and everyone knew that love was blind.

Fanny had expected Sir Charles to accompany his parents to the supper party—and so it was with dismay that she learned that he had not yet returned home. Only Squire Deveney and his wife were to be the guests.

Still . . . she must do her best to please these future in-laws, for Fanny had made up her romantic mind that she was to marry Sir Charles.

On the morning of the important day she escaped to the kitchens to have a gossip with Mrs Friendly, the cook, and found a new butler busy showing the footman how to polish a quantity of gold plate.

'Is that really gold?' asked Fanny, goggling at the glittering plates and knives and forks. Mrs Friendly drew her aside. 'It's only for this evening, Miss Fanny,' she whispered, 'as is that jackanapes of a butler. *He* was lured over from Lord Tandy's for the day. Lord Tandy is on the Grand Tour, and it's my guess that's his lordship's gold plate, for it came with his butler and goes back with his butler when the supper is over.'

'But why such trouble to entertain the Deveneys?' asked Fanny curiously. 'I seem to recall someone saying they were not at all well-heeled.'

Mrs Friendly folded her plump red arms across her starched apron. 'I think it is all for your benefit, Miss Fanny.'

'Me?'

'Seems the son, Sir Charles, made a great deal of prize money in the wars and your parents are anxious to make a match between you. With the Deveney family having such expectations, the master and mistress don't want to look poor.'

'No, I suppose not.' Fanny felt uneasy. Part of the romance about Sir Charles was that she had believed him to be as poor as herself. She had always been aware that her lack of dowry made her singularly unmarriageable.

Her hopes of Sir Charles as a future husband received a further blow when his

6

parents walked into the drawing room that evening. Mrs Deveney, a thin, dried-up-looking woman with sharp features and sandy hair was bedecked in diamonds. A diamond tiara glittered on her dusty hair and diamonds blazed at her withered neck. The squire was not the bluff John Bull of Fanny's imaginings but a sly-looking man like a horse dealer.

But she was bewildered by their praise of her—her gown, her hair, her beauty. Fanny glanced surreptitiously at a mirror over the fireplace and was startled to see that, to her, she looked much the same as ever.

Then they summoned their servant to bring in a picture of their son. Fanny, who had been expecting to see a miniature, was startled when a full-sized canvas was carried in and unveiled. 'This was painted by one of his officers,' said Mrs Deveney proudly. 'A most talented young man.'

The picture was unveiled. The servant carried forward a candelabrum. Fanny gazed on that picture and all her nagging doubts and fears about a borrowed butler and borrowed gold plate melted away. Here was the very stuff of dreams. The picture portrayed a young cavalry officer on a rearing white charger, a drawn sword in his hand. He had midnight black hair and a strong, rather cruel face. Behind him tumbled an approaching thunderstorm. Round about him lay the dead bodies of French soldiers. She had

7

remembered Sir Charles as having fair hair, but perhaps it had darkened later in life.

Fanny drew a deep breath and her eyes sparkled. 'A splendid-looking man!' exclaimed Mrs Page. 'Do you not think so, Fanny?'

And Fanny clasped her hands and murmured an ecstatic, 'Yes.'

Supper was a great success. Fanny was not expected to say much and so was free to dream more dreams. But to her surprise, as soon as supper was over, Mrs Page smiled on her indulgently and said, 'It has been a tiring day for you, Fanny. Why do you not retire?'

Too well schooled by that excellent Bath seminary to do anything so vulgar as to argue with her parents in public, Fanny curtsied and withdrew. She had no lady's maid and so she put herself to bed, dreaming all the while of the handsome and dashing Sir Charles.

The Deveneys and Pages had retired back to the drawing room. They settled themselves comfortably and then looked at one another in an amiable, almost telepathic silence, broken finally by the squire, who rubbed his hands together with a dry sound like sandpaper and said, 'Fine gal, your Fanny. A treasure.'

'Exactly,' said Mr Page.

'Glad to see you in such comfortable circumstances,' pursued the squire.

'Yes,' said Mrs Page, with affected languor. 'Such a windfall when Aunt Isobel died and left me her fortune.'

'I think you know what is in our minds.' The squire hitched his chair forward.

'Ah!' Mrs Page looked arch. 'I do believe you wish our Fanny for your Charles.'

'Demme, the lady's a genius.' Mrs Deveney nodded vigorously and set the diamonds on her head shimmering and sparkling.

'When does Sir Charles return?' asked Mr Page. He was normally a jolly, plump man, but for this special occasion his rotund form had been lashed into an Apollo corset, and, as he had eaten too much at dinner, felt he might burst at any moment.

'In a month's time. Good lad. Anxious to settle down,' said the squire.

'And Fanny will, of course, be guided by us,' said Mrs Page.

They all beamed at one another.

'As to the question of the marriage settlements,' said the squire, and the Pages perceptibly stiffened, wondering how on earth they were going to raise the wind for Fanny's dowry. 'Call me an old romantic,' said the squire, sighing and putting his hand on his heart, 'but I'm set on a love match and I don't want these young things to have their lives clouded by financial arrangements, not until after the wedding, that is.'

Had it not been for Mrs Deveney's splendid diamonds, the Pages might have become suspicious, but as it was, neither of them could take their eyes off those sparkling gems for long.

'Our feelings entirely,' said Mr Page. His brain seemed to him to be working at a great rate. They could rent the house and leave for the Continent immediately after the wedding—and stay away until the Deveneys got used to the fact that there was no money forthcoming.

'In that case,' he said, 'when do you plan to hold the wedding?'

'On the day after Charles returns,' said the squire.

For the first time, Mrs Page experienced a qualm of conscience. 'But—but Fanny should at least have an opportunity to become acquainted with him first.'

'No need for that. Young people. Well suited. Charles will do as he's told.'

Mr and Mrs Page argued a little for the sake of form, but terror of letting the prize slip through their fingers finally made them agree to everything. The squire said that their respective lawyers would get together a week after the wedding. Champagne was produced. The squire privately thought it was the oddest champagne he had ever tasted, which was perhaps the case, the 'champagne' being apple juice laced with soda water.

They fell to discussing arrangements. The couple would be married in the local church by the vicar. The Pages asked about a honeymoon, neither of them wanting to be around when their daughter and her new husband found they had rented Delfton Hall and disappeared.

'I'll fix that,' said the squire. 'Have you ever met my wife's unmarried sister, Miss Martha Grimes?'

'Didn't even know you had a sister-in-law,' commented Mr Page.

'She's got a house in the best part of town. We'll send 'em there for a few weeks. I'll write and tell her they're coming.' The squire put the knowledge that his sister-in-law had called him a loose screw and had told him never to cross her threshold again to the back of his mind.

It was four in the morning before the Deveneys took their leave—unaware that the gold plate and the butler had departed to their rightful home at midnight. The Pages had few remaining servants, the cook, Mrs Friendly, acting as housekeeper as well. She stayed on because her son had been allowed the use of the kitchen garden, the produce of which she sold to the neighboring houses.

In their carriage on the road home, Squire Deveney said to his wife, 'Better get those sparklers back to the jeweller in the morning. They did their bit.'

'Did you see how they gazed at my diamonds?' crowed his wife.

'Not *your* diamonds. Only on loan,' the squire reminded her.

'Don't be so depressing,' snapped his wife.

11

'We've done well for Charles. That gold plate was worth a king's ransom. We'll rent the house and clear off right after the wedding. But where?'

'Beat Tommy Wellan at cards before we left London,' said the squire, rubbing his hands, 'Said I'd waive the money if he let us use that hunting box of his in Yorkshire. 'Course, all I was thinking of at the time was escaping the duns.'

Mrs Deveney nodded toward the rewrapped portrait on the opposite carriage seat. 'Be a bit of a shock to the girl when she realizes Charles don't look like that at all. Who is it?'

'How should I know? Some felon was trying to sell it down Barminster way in the Dog and Duck. He thought he saw the constable, so I got it for a song, he was so anxious to be rid of it. We'll make sure she don't see Charles until they're both at the altar.'

'But the wedding rehearsal . . .?'

'Don't need one. I'll get the vicar to guide them through the responses.'

His wife patted his hand. 'You think of everything.'

*   *   *

'There's one thing that nags me,' said Mr Page as he placed a red Kilmarnock nightcap on his head and climbed into the high four-poster beside his wife. 'Why did they agree so readily

12

to meeting our lawyers *after* the marriage? I mean, if they're that rich, they could do better for their son.'

'It's our one chance of a good marriage for Fanny,' said his wife practically. 'If you have doubts, just think of those Deveney diamonds! Not to mention Charles's prize money. No, my dear, we are very lucky.'

*   *   *

Fanny was alarmed, not delighted, to learn that she was to marry Sir Charles without any opportunity of seeing much of him before the wedding, the Pages not knowing the Deveneys' plan of keeping their son away from Fanny until the very day of the wedding.

But romance and imagination warred with common sense, and romance and imagination won. Now, from that portrait, she knew what he looked like. She had someone to dream about. Sir Charles in her dreams made such marvelous, such dizzying speeches of undying love that Fanny hardly lived one moment in reality as she was fitted for a trousseau, largely consisting of her mother's made-over gowns. Fanny herself was an expert needlewoman and studied the fashion magazines, so she altered a great number of the already altered gowns to a more fashionable line.

She did, however, voice the idea that it was a pity there was no miniature of her to send to

13

her betrothed, whereupon her mother gave a merry laugh and called her a forgetful puss, saying that a miniature of her had been taken the year before by a very competent artist. Fanny pointed out she had never sat for her portrait, but Mrs Page had an answer ready. The artist had been brilliant but eccentric and had been placed next to the drawing room, where he had covertly studied her in order to do the miniature.

Which all made Mrs Page throughly pleased that she had succumbed to temptation in London and had stolen a little miniature of the reigning belle, Miss Woodward, while she and her husband were guests at a party at the Woodwards' home. She had not taken it because she was fascinated with the features of the beauty but because the little frame had been encrusted with gems. The gems had been prised out, so that the sale from them would furnish the Pages with funds to escape abroad after the wedding, and the miniature packaged and sent to the barracks in Bristol to await Sir Charles's return. Miss Woodward was divinely fair, with large blue eyes, and did not look at all like Fanny, but as Mrs Page said to her husband, 'All's fair in love and war. Get him to the altar. That's all that matters.'

The thing that puzzled Fanny was that they did not see the Deveneys. Messages were sent back and forth between the two families, but the Deveneys did not visit the Pages and the

Pages did not call on the Deveneys—and Fanny was not to know that neither family wanted to go to any further expense in keeping up appearances of being rich.

Knowing how gossip traveled easily in country districts, Mrs Page had paid the cook, Mrs Friendly, and had told her of the mythical legacy from Aunt Isobel but had sworn her to secrecy, knowing Mrs Friendly to be a chatterbox. Mrs Friendly had told her son— she was unusual in an age when servants were not supposed to marry, but had been taken on by the Pages, who could not afford to be over nice in such matters—and her son had got drunk down at the Dog and Duck and had confided in his best friend, Gully Simpson, who was walking out with the vicar's scullery maid, and so the news went the rounds and joined up with the gossip from the Deveney camp about Sir Charles returning from the wars, loaded down with prize money and loot—so loaded down that it was taking a separate ship to bring his wealth home.

And in the middle of all this gossip and speculation moved the small figure of Fanny Page, lost in dreams of that handsome, harsh man on his white charger.

*   *   *

There was one man whom Lord Gilbert Bohun loathed with every fibre of his being, and that man was Sir Charles Deveney. Lord Gilbert smoldered beside the fire in the officers' mess at Bristol and covertly studied his 'enemy.' Sir Charles Deveney was slight and fair. He had fine grey eyes in a clever, sensitive face and looked almost too delicate to be an officer. But he had been knighted for bravery, and what was more, was adored by every man in the regiment, who jumped to attention every time they saw him, whereas Lord Bohun was regarded with dislike. The fact that he was cruel, that he led his regiment from behind whenever possible, did not cross Lord Bohun's mind. His jealousy of Sir Charles festered and burned. To add to Lord Bohun's bad humor, a letter had been waiting for him from his factor to say that the portrait of his lordship on a white charger with drawn sword, commissioned at great expense by his lordship from a Spanish artist and shipped home, had failed to arrive, the coach that was carrying it from Bristol to Lord Bohun's home in Gloucestershire having been held up by footpads.

He noticed that Sir Charles was staring at a letter as if he could not believe his eyes and sourly hoped it was bad news.

Sir Charles read the letter from his father for the second time. Squire Deveney had written that a marriage had been arranged for Charles with Miss Fanny Page, aged seventeen. The family' fortunes were at low ebb. In fact, the squire wrote touchingly, if Charles did not go through with this wedding, then the Deveneys would end their days in a debtors' prison.

Sir Charles had been looking forward to a well-deserved leave. He longed to relax at home, get in a bit of shooting, a bit of fishing, but thoughts of the fair sex had not entered his mind. Unlike most of his fellow officers, he had learned to manage on his army pay, which he augmented cleverly from time to time with wins at the card table, having learned that if you stuck to water when all about you were getting drunk, chances were of winning hands down every time.

He sensed a lightening of the atmosphere in the room and realized Lord Bohun had left. The man's dislike of him was a constant irritation to Sir Charles.

He picked up a small package that had also been waiting for his arrival and tore off the wrapping. It was a miniature with a covering letter from his future father-in-law. 'You probably do not remember our Fanny,' Mr Page had written, 'but she has grown to extreme beauty.' The rest of the letter contained fulsome compliments and best wishes for 'the happy couple'.

Sir Charles opened up the leather case containing the miniature. The beauty of the face looking up at him made him catch his breath. So stunning was that beauty that he did not notice the rather scarred edges of the miniature, where the gems had been gouged out.

The door opened and his fellow officer, Capt. Tommy Hawkes, walked in. 'Morning, Major,' he said, sinking into an armchair opposite. 'News from home?'

'Very startling news,' said Sir Charles. 'My impoverished parents have decided to recoup the family losses by marrying me off.'

'To whom?'

'To a neighbor's daughter, Miss Fanny Page, only seventeen years old, but evidently very rich.'

'No harm in that,' said Tommy. 'Marry this heiress, enjoy your leave, kiss her good-bye, and return to the wars.'

'How would you feel about kissing *this* goodbye?' Sir Charles passed him the miniature.

Tommy let out a soundless whistle. 'You've landed on your feet, Major. A face to die for.'

Sir Charles took the miniature back from him. 'Yes,' he said slowly. 'But why should parents of a rich heiress want her to marry me? They've only to take a dazzler like that to London and she could have the pick of the bunch.'

'Don't question fortune,' said Tommy. 'I'd like to see you with more of the readies. Can't stand the way Bohun sneers at you the whole time and flaunts his wealth in front of you.'

'We won't have to suffer Bohun any longer. He's sold out. I won't be plagued with him again.'

'But are you really going to marry this girl, just like that? It's up to you. Your parents can't force you. Remember, those miniatures can be misleading. Do you remember Carter of the Forty-fifth? Got a miniature of a dazzler, fell in love, rushed back home on his first leave, and found she had teeth like a rabbit and a squint.'

'Well, we'll see. Time I settled down. Never thought I would have the money to do it. You know, I am well aware that it's the fashion, but there's something about getting wed to a female for her money that sticks in my craw. But my parents appear to be heading for the debtors' prison this time and that does not surprise me in the least. They make me feel like a hundred years old, they are so heedless and feckless. Money runs through their fingers like water. Will you be my best man?'

Tommy looked gratified. 'I would be honored. When do we leave?'

Sir Charles studied the letter again. 'This is ridiculous! They have arranged the wedding for next Monday! We'll need to travel hard to get there in time. What are they thinking of? I hope this is not some heiress who has become pregnant by the stable boy and needs a husband.'

'You can always say no,' Tommy pointed

19

out.

'With the limited time I have to get there, it looks as if I will only see this female at the altar and in front of the vicar.'

'So, you tip me the wink and when they get to the part about anyone having just cause to stop the marriage, I'll cry out that you're already wed to a senorita in Spain,' said Tommy.

Sir Charles grinned. 'That should do the trick. Pity I don't look like the awful Bohun. There isn't much about me for a lady to dream about.'

Tommy studied the clever, sensitive face, the large grey eyes, the firm mouth and chin, and the slender athlete's body opposite him. 'You'll do,' he said gruffly. 'The men would follow you to hell and back, and they wouldn't do that for Bohun.'

Sir Charles sighed. 'But would the ladies even follow me across the street? Never mind. Let us get packed.'

CHAPTER TWO

On the evening of her wedding day, Fanny slipped down to the kitchen to have a quiet talk with Mrs Friendly. Everything was ready, everything prepared. Her wedding gown stood like a mute white ghost on a stand in the

20

corner of her room.

There had been no opportunity for walks, for sensible thought, or for talks in the kitchen because of pinnings and fittings and alterations.

Mrs Friendly was seated at the scrubbed wooden table, her cap askew, purple bruises of fatigue under her eyes. 'Don't reckon as when I've baked so much this age, Miss Fanny,' she said wearily. 'But you'll have a wedding breakfast a queen would be proud of.'

Fanny sat down opposite the cook. 'I am a trifle frightened,' she said candidly. 'I know the appearance of my intended but not his disposition. He could be a brute.'

'Not Charles Deveney,' said the cook, 'though I haven't seen him this age. I remember him as a lad. Gentle soul. Very quiet.'

'The army ... the wars ... must change people.'

'Don't know that it does, Miss Fanny. Fact is, it's just another hunting field for the likes of them. You'll be getting a house of your own. You'll like that. And children will come along. There's a lot to be said for being married—and nothing at all for being a spinster ... not unless you're a very rich spinster.'

'What I find most peculiar,' said Fanny, resting her chin on her hands, 'is that Baxter, the Deveneys' odd man, was in the village this afternoon. He bowed and wished me well and

21

said it was good to have Sir Charles home again. He arrived this morning. Now would you not think he would wish to ride over and *see* me?'

Mrs Friendly, who knew of Sir Charles's arrival, had indeed thought just that, but kindness made her say, 'It's by way of being an arranged marriage, and all the better for that. Love don't last.'

'But—but I have been dreaming about him. Seeing his face everywhere.' Fanny looked across at the shining row of copper pans as if seeing reflections of Sir Charles. 'It would be quite dreadful if he loved me and I did not love him.'

'Hush now. Everything will be well. You'd best get off to bed and get a good night's sleep.'

'But I do not think I can sleep. There are the intimacies of marriage I wish to learn about.'

'You should ask your mama.'

'Ma just turns a funny color and says ladies don't ask such questions.'

'Wouldn't worry about it,' said Mrs Friendly, deciding it was better for Fanny not to know what awaited her. 'Just a lot of kissing and cuddling.'

'Heavens! Is *that* all? And that's how ladies have babies?'

'Sure as sure.'

'Well, when I walked into the kitchen last

week—you did not see me—but you were being hugged and kissed by the blacksmith. Mrs Friendly, does that mean . . .?'

'All right for me,' said Mrs Friendly defensively. 'My poor Jim's been in his grave this age.'

'But are you going to have another child?'

'Gracious, no!'

'But you said . . .'

'I'm too old. Only happens to young girls.'

'Oh. I think I can cope with kissing and cuddling. It might be quite pleasant.'

'Very pleasant, miss. And nothing for you to worry your head about.'

Somewhat comforted, Fanny retired upstairs to her bedchamber. But that night she dreamed of the Sir Charles in the picture. His face was dark with spite and rage and he was advancing on her with his fists clenched. She awoke with a scream. She lay awake for a few moments. In the light of the rushlight by her bed, she could dimly make out the white glimmering shape of her wedding gown. What if she took one look at Sir Charles and loathed him? She could run from the church. But where to? She had no money. When she had been at the seminary with the other, richer girls, the talk had all been of first Seasons, and killing glances, and flirtations, and she had joined in, thinking somehow that she, too, was destined for a London Season. It had been a cold awakening to find there was no prospect of a Season, no balls and parties to look forward to. Perhaps Sir Charles would take her to balls and parties. After all, things were not so bad. She was going to London at last—and surely Sir Charles would take her to some of the entertainments. That vicious face faded from her mind, replaced by a tender and admiring one, and she fell into a dreamless sleep.

*   *   *

Sir Charles, in morning dress—there had been no time or money to order a suit of wedding clothes—waited nervously at the altar in the church of St Edmund's for his bride.

Beside him stood Tommy Hawkes, a thin bean pole of a man with large feet. Tommy thought it was all very jolly and unpretentious. The church was bedecked with evergreens, just like Christmas, and filled with country people. He was surprised there were no gentry, only the Deveneys and Mrs Page with their servants. The vicar, the Reverend Percival Thwyte-Simpson, looked just like a vicar should look with his venerable snowy locks and rosy cheeks.

The village band up in the gallery was playing a jaunty selection of hymns in double-quick time. Outside, pale spring sunlight was flooding the countryside and striking down through the old stained glass of the windows

24

and on the silent marble tombs of braver Pages and more honorable Deveneys. The church, however, was very cold. Tommy could feel his first British chilblain beginning to itch and the tip of his long nose turning red.

Sir Charles stood very still and erect, as if on the parade ground. He was wishing his bride would hurry up. The whole thing seemed unreal.

Odd things had happened the night before. The Deveneys' elderly footman had welcomed him home and had said, 'Blessings on your return, Sir Charles. There must be carriages and carriages due to arrive with all the spoils of victory.' Sir Charles had laughed happily, thinking the old man was making a joke, and deciding later he had been serious. But everyone expected soldiers to come home dripping with the spoils of war. And why had he not been allowed to see his bride? He could not even get a description of her from his parents. What if she were a fright? Or worse, a shrew?

And then there was a rustling behind him and the band settled down to play a measured march.

Fanny looked down the church. A slight, fair man was standing where a tall, dark one should have been. Her step faltered. 'That is not Sir Charles,' she murmured to her father.

'Wedding nerves,' he said, patting her arm. 'It's Sir Charles all right.'

Numb with cold and nerves, Fanny went to stand beside him.

Sir Charles looked at her, at the glossy black curls under the coronet of pearls, and the wide eyes and elfin face. Veils were unfashionable that year, so he was able to see her clearly. Not the face of the miniature, but dainty and appealing. He let out a little sigh of relief. It could have been much worse.

The opening speech of the wedding ceremony slid in and out Fanny's worried brain. Why was this man so very different from the portrait?

The voice of the vicar interrupted her thoughts. '"... and therefore it is not by any to be enterprised, nor taken in hand, unadvisedly, lightly, or wantonly, to satisfy men's carnal lusts and appetites, like brute beasts that have no understanding . . ."'

Goodness, thought Fanny, I never really heard the words before. Carnal lusts, indeed!

The vicar read on. '"It was ordained for a remedy against sin, and to avoid fornication; that such persons as have not the gift of continency might marry, and keep themselves undefiled . . ."'

Nothing like the *Book of Common Prayer* for calling a spade a spade, thought Sir Charles.

He sensed Fanny's worry and distress. How awful, he thought, that such a young girl should be seeing the man she is to spend the rest of her life with for the first time. It's like being sold into slavery!

And then the vicar's voice pierced his worried thoughts again.

'"I require and charge you both, as ye will answer at the dreadful day of judgment when the secrets of all hearts shall be disclosed, that if either of you know of any impediment, why ye may not be lawfully joined together in Matrimony, ye do now confess it."'

Tommy nudged him. Sir Charles glanced down at the endearing face beside him and remained silent. Fanny half opened her mouth. She wanted to cry out that she had been tricked, that this was not the man she had promised she would marry, but fear kept her silent and the ceremony went on . . . and on. She promised to love and obey, she heard exhortations reminding her that she was the 'weaker vessel' and must be 'faithful and obedient to her husband; and in all quietness, sobriety and peace, be a follower of holy and godly matrons.'

And then it was over. She was Lady Charles Deveney. She smiled blindly to right and left as she walked down the aisle on the arm of her husband. Lucy Partington, a faded spinster of the parish enjoying this day of glory bedecked in white muslin, held up her train. Fanny had wanted one of her friends from the seminary to be invited but had been told that Lucy would be deeply disappointed, which had surprised her, for she had been sure that in the past her parents had refused to have anything to do with the Partingtons, damning them as genteel poor—as if their own straitened circumstances were of a higher order.

She sat in the open wedding carriage next to her husband for the short drive to Delfton Hall. She wanted to say something, even if it was only, How do you do? Or, Hasn't the weather turned cold? But the words seemed to be frozen inside her and Sir Charles was looking worried and abstracted.

He said his first words directly to her as they entered the hall and he saw trunk after trunk piled up. 'What a trousseau! Is that all yours?'

'N-no,' said Fanny. 'I have two trunks of clothes and two bandboxes. There they are over there. How odd! My mother and father must be going somewhere, but they said nothing of it to me.'

'No gold plates,' remarked Mrs Deveney at the wedding breakfast.

'Low people here,' said the squire. 'Probably didn't want it stolen. We'll be all right. We'll stay away for a year. By that time the heir will surely be on the way and we'll be able to claim we lost our fortune in the intervening time. They should have their own grand establishment by then. We'll move in on 'em and live like kings for the rest of our lives.'

'Pretty wedding,' said Mrs Page, 'although I must say Sir Charles doesn't look a bit like his portrait.'

'Well, Fanny don't look like that miniature you sent. Hey, could it be that the Deveneys are playing the same game?' her husband exclaimed.

'Look at them,' said Mrs Page comfortably, nodding toward the Deveneys. 'Not a brain between the pair of them. All will be well. We'll stay abroad until we're sure a child is on the way and then we'll just move in on them.'

Sir Charles wanted to speak to his father. The squire was across the table from him at the wedding breakfast, but every time he tried to catch his attention, to signal to him that he wished to be private with him, the squire appeared not to see and immediately began to talk to Mrs Deveney.

Still, no doubt this new wife of his could explain a lot. They were to spend the first night of their marriage at an expensive posting house on the road to London, where they were to stay with Aunt Martha.

He exchanged a few remarks with her about the guests, about the weather, and she answered in monosyllables and picked at her food.

Fanny had lived in her mind for the past weeks with that tall, dark man of the portrait. She was bewildered. She could not adjust to the fact that this fair-haired man who looked younger than his years was her husband. But he looked kind, and certainly not at all threatening. She looked around at the guests.

It was surely unusual for her parents to invite so many country folk, farmers, and shopkeepers to grace their table. She did not know her parents had not invited any of the local gentry or aristocracy for fear that they might gossip to the Deveneys about the Pages' notorious lack of wealth.

There was to be no dancing after the breakfast, no festivities. Fanny, followed by the twittering and excited Miss Partington, went up to her room for the last time, where a housemaid helped Miss Partington remove Fanny's wedding gown and attire her instead in a modish carriage gown of blue velvet.

Fanny kept looking toward the bedroom door, expecting her mother to arrive for a few last words, but Mrs Page did not appear.

When she descended to the hall, she could see through the open doors that the light was already beginning to fade. A post chaise waited outside. For some reason neither the Pages nor the Deveneys had wished to part with their traveling carriages. Sir Charles was waiting for her. He smiled and patted her hand in a reassuring way and she smiled tremulously at him.

Her mother stood well back behind the guests as Fanny was helped into the post chaise. A ragged cheer went up and then they were off. Man and wife. Off to an unknown future.

'Well, that went quite well,' said Sir Charles.

He had a light, pleasant voice.

'Yes,' said Fanny in a small voice. 'I thought—I thought you might have made an effort to—to see me before the wedding.'

'I was told you did not wish it,' he said. 'I confess I thought it most odd. I hope, however, you are not disappointed in me.'

She was, terribly, but could not bring herself to say so.

It was all too much. 'If you don't mind,' she said in a little voice, 'I would like to sleep.'

'Go ahead,' he said amiably, and Fanny closed her eyes tightly and affected to fall asleep—until the affectation became reality and she slept neatly and soundly until he at last awoke her and told her they had arrived at the posting house, where they were to spend the night.

She walked up the broad staircase with him, behind the landlord, who was singing the praises of his 'best room'. She waited while their trunks were carried in, looking all the while at the large fourposter bed as if it were an instrument of torture.

Sir Charles tipped the servants, the landlord bowed and withdrew, and the couple were alone.

Fanny stood very still, staring at the floor. Sir Charles gently removed her hat. She still stood there.

He thought he really ought to begin by kissing her. But she looked so odd, so frozen with fright. He knew that virgins were expected to be frozen with fright, but it did seem, on the other hand, a bit hard to drag a girl off to bed with whom he had only exchanged a few pleasantries. He remembered she had only eaten very little at the breakfast, which, like most wedding breakfasts, had been at three in the afternoon. So he pushed open a door at the side of the bedroom and said, 'Look, we have a private parlor. What do you say to a little supper first?'

'Yes,' said Fanny eagerly, anxious to stave off the terrifying moment when she would need to undress in front of this stranger.

He opened the door and shouted for the waiter—and after ordering supper suggested they should wait in the parlor beside the fire.

The little parlor was brightly lit with beeswax candles. It must be a very expensive place to have beeswax candles instead of tallow, thought Fanny, and then was relieved to remember that her parents had arranged all this and had paid the bill in advance.

'Would you like to change out of your carriage dress?' asked Sir Charles, but Fanny, feeling armored in thick blue velvet, shook her head.

'I think we should start by getting to know each other,' said Sir Charles. He looked at the little elfin creature who was sitting on the very edge of the chair opposite him. 'You are not at all like your miniature,' he said.

Those huge eyes of hers flew up to meet his. 'Oh, the one Mama sent you. I never saw it. She said the artist was most eccentric and took my likeness while studying me covertly from another room.'

'Then the fool must have drawn one of your friends. Here! Let me show it to you.' He fished in his pocket, took out the miniature in its leather case, and passed it to her.

'But this is ridiculous!' she exclaimed. 'This is not me! What has happened? Are both our parents mad? It looks as little like me as did that portrait supposed to be of you that your parents showed me.'

'But no one has ever painted my portrait!'

'It was of a dark, handsome man on a white charger.'

'What is going on?' He looked at her in bewilderment. Then his face grew grim. 'I am beginning to fear that my parents may have done everything to trap you into marriage with me.'

'But why?' wailed Fanny. 'What is wrong with you? With all that prize money you could marry anyone you wanted.'

'I have no prize money. I have only my army pay.'

Fanny looked at him, stricken. 'I thought you knew that,' he said. 'My dear, I am afraid my parents were after your money.'

She looked at him, bewildered. 'But I have no money. Your parents said you were returning home with a shipload of loot . . . and your mama was bedecked in diamonds when I saw her.'

'My mother does not possess diamonds. You have no money?'

'No, I doubt if I even have a dowry.'

'Gulled like the veriest flat,' he said bitterly. 'Now, what are we going to do?'

At that moment the waiters entered with their supper. Both ate and drank silently until the covers were removed and the servants left.

He leaned back in his chair and surveyed her. 'We can live on my pay,' he said, 'but it will be difficult, especially if there are children.'

Tears welled up in Fanny's eyes. 'I thought I was going to have some fun at last,' she said. 'I thought we would go to balls and parties. I have never been to London.'

'If only we could put the clock back,' he said. 'If only we had found out any of this before we got married. Don't cry. I'm damned if I'll let them get away with this. You're so young. You should have had a Season and lots of fellows to choose from.'

Fanny cried quietly over her glass of unaccustomed wine. She had never been allowed anything stronger than lemonade before and had even drunk the toasts at her wedding in lemonade.

'Look here,' he said gently, 'this will not do at all. I shall go downstairs and get a horse and ride home. Our parents must not be allowed to

34

get away with this. Give me a few moments to change into my riding clothes and then you can go to bed.'

After he had gone into the bedroom, Fanny dried her tears and blew her nose firmly. It was every bit as bad for him as it was for her. He was not a brute or a monster.

When he returned, she gave him a watery smile. 'I am behaving like the veriest weakling,' she said.

'Never mind. Wait for me. Thank goodness I do not have very far to ride.'

*   *   *

When he reached his home, he hammered on the door until he heard a faint answering shout, then a window on the ground floor opened and the elderly footman looked out.

'I wish to see my parents,' said Sir Charles.

'They've gone, sir. Wait a bit. I'll unbolt the door.'

Sir Charles heard his shuffling footsteps approach the door, saw the candle that he carried bobbing along the line of windows.

The footman opened the door and he stepped into the hall. 'Gone? What do you mean, gone?'

'It's as much a surprise to me, sir, as it was to you. We thought all those trunks was your treasure. Gone to Yorkshire or somewheres like that and strangers coming here next week

35

to rent the house.'

'What about Mr Hawkes?'

'Reckon he was surprised as anyone else, sir. Went off to London.'

'I had best go and see my in-laws,' said Sir Charles grimly. 'They have a lot of explaining to do.'

But at the Pages, he roused Mrs Friendly, who told him that the Pages had gone abroad, gone just like that, and had rented *their* house, servants and all, to a Mr Robinson, due to arrive to take up residence in two weeks' time.

'Is Lady Charles well?' asked the cook, still bewildered at all the changes—and at the sight of the bridegroom on his wedding night, standing glaring at her as if he could not believe his ears.

'Yes, very well,' he said abruptly. 'Why was nothing of this told to me? My parents have gone as well.'

'I am sure I don't know, sir. Have you come far? Would you care for a glass of wine?'

'No. On second thoughts, yes. I must think.'

Soon he was seated in the drawing room with a decanter of port. He turned the facts over in his mind. It was all very plain. His parents thought they were tricking the Pages and getting him an heiress. The Pages had thought they were tricking the Deveneys and that he really did have prize money. So they had seen to it that he had married Fanny—and then had left to avoid any repercussions.

How could he have been such a fool? Fanny's predicament was understandable. She had thought she was gaining a rich and handsome husband. But after the wars and the carnage, he had thought naively he was returning to the innocence of home. He had believed his parents when they had told him that this marriage of his was necessary to save them from the debtors' prison and that Fanny's dowry would be their salvation. He could cope with it, as he had coped with so much already in his life. He liked Fanny. She was an endearing little thing. She should have been giggling at balls and parties and dreaming of beaux. Was Aunt Martha part of this plot? He had not seen her in years, but remembered her as being a rather grim and upright spinster. No, Aunt Martha would know nothing of this, and then with a sinking heart, he remembered her strong disapproval of his parents. He was beginning to think his aunt knew nothing of their impending arrival.

And then the words of Tommy Hawkes drifted into his worried mind. Tommy was fond of saying that to cut a dash in London society, one had to have a great deal of money, or, failing that, persuade society that one actually had a great deal of money. 'If society thinks you are very rich,' Tommy had said, 'then you can dine at other people's houses and have endless credit.'

The marriage had not been announced in

the newspapers. Only the locals knew of it, the servants and the vicar. London society would not. He thought of the weary years of living within his army pay, envying such men as Bohun their wealth. He began to feel that same reckless, heady sensation he had just before going into battle. He was accounted rich, was he? Then let London society think so. He would outdo his parents by living on credit, present Fanny as his cousin, and give her all the balls and parties she desired. It should be easy to get an annullment if the marriage were not consummated.

The first thing was to erase any record of that marriage from the parish register. The local church was small but accounted very fine. It often had visitors. He tossed off his glass of wine and let himself out of the house. He swung himself into the saddle and rode off toward the church. He seemed to have left all his ideas of thrift and moral rectitude behind. Had he not found a window in the vestry unlatched, then he knew he would have shot the lock in the door and stolen something from the church to hide the real intention of his visit.

The moon was striking down into the vestry, which smelled of damp hassocks, oil heaters, and incense. He swung open the heavy register. There was his name and signature and that of Fanny's on top of a fresh page. He took out a penknife and sliced out the page, carefully slitting it as far in as he could manage so that there would not be immediate visible evidence of his crime.

A small voice of reason somewhere in the back of his head was telling him that he was behaving ridiculously, that he could not expect to get away with his outrageous plan, that should Fanny find the man of her dreams in London, it was going to be hard to keep a marriage quiet until they got an annullment. The normally sensible Sir Charles was revolted by his parents' behavior.

He crumpled up the page of the register and put it in his pocket before riding back to the posting house. The bedroom was in darkness. He lit a candle, drew back the bed curtains, and looked down at his sleeping wife. There were marks of tears on her cheeks. He gave a little sigh. He was suddenly very tired and did not want to sleep in the one hard chair before the fire.

He undressed quickly and slipped into bed beside her. She yawned and murmured something in her sleep and snuggled up against him. Sudden desire coursed through his body and he edged away. He had not had a woman in too long a time. But he could not spoil the chance of an annullment by taking her virginity.

*   *   *

Fanny awoke and stared up at the bed canopy, wondering for a brief second where she was. Then memory came flooding back. Soft breathing on the pillow next to her own made her stiffen. She twisted her head and looked into the sleeping features of her husband. His nightcap had fallen off and his thick, fair hair was ruffled, making him look young and vulnerable. He had more lace on his nightgown than she had on her own: a new nightgown, one obviously bought for his wedding night. Misery at her own situation was alleviated by a sudden sharp concern for his. He should have been lying next to a loving wife.

As if conscious of her gaze, he opened his eyes, looked at her for a long moment, and then smiled. She stiffened again, expecting him to reach for her, but he yawned and stretched and said, 'Goodness, I'm hungry. Couldn't eat much of that supper last night with all this worry. We'll have breakfast and I'll tell you my plans.'

He swung his legs out of bed, stood up, and pulled his nightgown over his head, revealing a well-muscled back marred by a long, puckered scar. After one brief, shy look, she turned away from him and lay with her eyes tight shut—until he said in an amused voice, 'Are you going to lie there all day, Fanny?'

'No, Sir Charles,' she said in a small voice. 'But I have never been in a bedroom with a gentleman before.'

'I should hope not. Call me Charles, Fanny. You get dressed and I'll go and order breakfast.'

She got up when he had closed the door behind him. Great waves of relief were flooding her. He had not tried to make love to her, he had not shouted or cursed her as he had every reason to do. She dressed quickly and then joined him in the parlor.

He waited until they both had eaten and the servants had retired, then said, 'We have indeed both been sadly tricked. Your parents and my parents, having gulled us, have both headed off for different points of the compass and left us destitute. I am not going to let them get away with this. You should marry the man of your choice. In fact, if I can pull this off, you shall.

'Now, no one knows we are married, no one in the gentry or aristocracy, that is. The marriage was not announced. I tore the page recording the marriage out of the register. We will go to London as cousins. If I can catch Tommy Hawkes before he starts talking about our wedding, I will get him to put about the fiction that we are both fabulously wealthy. We will be invited everywhere. You will have all the balls and parties you desire. As soon as you meet the man of your dreams, we will set about getting the marriage annulled.'

Fanny looked at him round-eyed. 'But the man of my dreams—as you call him—will

41

promptly shy off.'

'Not if he loves you.'

'And if I don't meet anyone?'

'Well, I'll think of something. Why should we not have a bit of fun?'

She wrinkled her brow and looked at him doubtfully. 'But what if someone from your regiment knows you, or their families? You cannot then maintain the fiction of prize money.'

'That's true. Lord Bohun has sold out and he hates me—and he certainly would explode any tale of prize money.'

Fanny smiled at him, suddenly liking him immensely and thinking he was very much like the brother she always wanted to have.

'I have it!' she cried. 'Say you have a relative, a nabob, left all his wealth to you. As for me, I will put it about that some merchant who owed Papa a favor left me all his moneybags.'

'That's my girl. And if it doesn't work out, we'll just need to put up with each other!'

CHAPTER THREE

Sir Charles and Fanny waited anxiously beside their trunks in the hall of Miss Martha Grimes's residence in Hanover Square. They had already been kept waiting half an hour.

'It's as I thought,' said Sir Charles gloomily. 'She was not even informed we were to visit her. And the fact that your parents had not paid the posting house bill is an insult. Don't look so depressed, Fanny. If she doesn't want us, we'll go and look for Tommy Hawkes and see if he can find us a place to stay.'

He looked up as the butler descended the stairs. 'Madam will see you now,' he said in the gloomy voice good servants use to impart to visitors that if they had any sense they would have known better than to call.

They followed him up the winding staircase and into a light, airy drawing room.

Martha Grimes rose as they entered the room and surveyed the pair with some surprise. Sir Charles looked like a fine young man from the top of his thick, fair hair to his shiny Hessian boots. She thought he had more the face of a scholar than an army man: clever and sensitive, with fine grey eyes.

His wife was a pretty little thing who looked half scared, half tired. But Miss Grimes hardened her heart. She had had more than enough of the sponging Deveneys. Through long years of being subjected to the wiles of adventurers and various grasping relatives, she had learned to keep the extent of her wealth a secret. She and her sister had received equal amounts of money in their parents' will. She had invested hers and made her money grow. Her sister had married Mr Deveney and managed to squander the lot in only two Seasons.

She was a tall, hard-featured woman of forty-five. She had thick, brown hair, without a trace of grey, under a starched cap. Her brown eyes were very dark, almost black, the kind of eyes that give nothing away.

'Sit down,' she said, 'and tell me why you are come . . . and why you think I should entertain you.'

Sir Charles, during his wait in the hall, had thought up all sorts of tales to tell her, but he suddenly decided that nothing less than the truth would do.

Miss Grimes heard him out as he told her everything, including his intention to masquerade as Fanny's cousin and pretend to be rich.

When he had finished at last, she fought down an unaccustomed desire to laugh. But she said sternly, 'I do not hold with cheating tradespeople. I will not have you living on credit.'

'But if we were thought to be very rich,' said Sir Charles patiently, 'we would spend most of the Season being entertained at other peoples' houses.'

'You would be lying . . . tricking people.'

'True, but only for a little, only until Fanny finds someone suitable.'

'And what is wrong with you?' asked Miss Grimes. She looked curiously at Fanny.

'Sir Charles is very kind, quite like a brother,' said Fanny. 'But it would be wonderful to have some fun, if only for a little.'

'Both of us are in need of some larks,' said Sir Charles. 'I am war-weary, and Fanny must not be denied a few pleasures because of her parents.'

'In order to maintain this fiction,' said Miss Grimes, 'I would need to support it in every detail—to help you with your lies, to chaperon Lady Deveney. Did you think of that?'

Fanny bent her head. 'No,' she whispered. 'I do not think we did.'

Sir Charles reached out, took her hand, and gave it a reassuring squeeze.

Was ever a pair so admirably matched, marveled Miss Grimes, and yet so determined not to be tricked any further that they do not realize it?

And what would this deception entail? It would mean an end of her lonely days for a little, it would mean going back into society, the society she had shunned for so long, which, in fact, had also shunned her, a middle-aged spinster not being considered at all interesting. Had she broadcast the extent of her present fortune, her life would have changed, but she had no desire to be a target of leeches and adventurers.

None of her thoughts showed on her face, a face well schooled over years of loneliness and rejection to mask hurt or worry.

Sir Charles gave a little sigh. Miss Grimes had a certain dignity and decency that made him feel guilty he had ever put such a shameful scheme to her. He rose. 'Come, Fanny,' he said.

Miss Grimes looked across at him. 'Sit down, young man,' she said. 'I haven't finished with you,' and sank back into a thoughtful silence.

The cries of the hawkers filtered through from the street below. A brewer's dray rumbled over the cobbles. The postman rang his bell. Inside the drawing room, a fire of sea coal spurted and flamed on the hearth.

'Very well,' said Miss Grimes, breaking her silence. 'From now on you are the rich Sir Charles and the rich Miss Fanny Page. Are you sure there is no one in London who knows of your wedding?'

'Only my friend, Tommy Hawkes, and he won't say anything.'

She tugged at the bell rope. 'You will be shown to your rooms. I advise you to rest; we shall meet at dinner and discuss this matter further.'

As the couple left, following the housekeeper, Miss Grimes noticed the way Fanny clung trustingly to Sir Charles's arm. Let the pair have a little fun. In a week's time, they would be in love.

*　　*　　*

46

Sir Charles visited Fanny's bedroom half an hour later. 'Is not Miss Grimes a treasure?' cried Fanny. 'We shall be so comfortable here. She is not at all what I expected. Not at all like your mama.'

'Had you not met her before?' asked Charles, stretching out on the bed and putting his hands behind his head.

'You should take off your boots,' chided Fanny, 'if you are going to lie on my bed.'

'Goodness, I'm tired,' Sir Charles said, yawning. 'You have definitely got the better bed, Fanny. Amazing soft.'

'Boots off,' said Fanny impatiently, and tugged off his Hessians and put them on the floor. 'I am just going to find a suitable dress for dinner and lay it out, then you must go off to your own bed because I want to sleep as well.'

He mumbled something indistinct. Fanny selected a sprigged muslin. The house was well fired, but the dining room might be cold, so she put a colorful Indian shawl beside it, kid gloves, thin kid slippers, the dress and shawl arranged on the chair and the slippers underneath, and then, satisfied, turned to say something to her husband and found he had fallen asleep.

She looked down at him and decided it would be cruel to awaken him, so she climbed in the other side of the bed, put her head against his arm, and cuddled against him and fell asleep as well.

Miss Grimes came in an hour later to see how Fanny was and stood for a moment watching the sleeping pair. This will not do at all, she thought. Sir Charles had given their names to the butler as Sir Charles Deveney and Miss Fanny Page. What on earth would the servants think if they found them in bed together?

She shook Sir Charles awake.

He looked up at her stern face and then twisted round to find his wife snuggled up against him. 'Oh. Lord,' he said. 'I am sorry. I fell asleep on her bed—and she is such an innocent, she probably saw nothing wrong in sleeping beside me.'

'Don't let it happen again,' whispered Miss Grimes severely.

*   *   *

Captain Tommy Hawkes was feeling ill done by. Like Sir Charles, he lived on his army pay. He was a younger son, so his family home and estates had gone to his elder brother, who did not encourage visitors. Tommy had been hoping for a pleasant stay with Sir Charles's parents. He had not expected to be sent packing by the Deveneys immediately after the wedding. He was staying at Limmer's Hotel in Bond Street—and had just been thinking

48

gloomily that he had better face up to the fact that he could not afford to be on leave for much longer and had better rejoin his regiment—when a footman arrived with a letter summoning him to dinner at the home of Miss Martha Grimes. He remembered that the lady was Charles's spinster aunt, and where the married couple was staying, and brightened at the thought of seeing his friend again.

He brushed and cleaned his dress uniform—glad that he never put on any weight, for he could not afford a new one—and then with his brown hair pomaded and his large feet in pumps, carefully painted to conceal the cracks of age, he set out to walk to Hanover Square, happy that the day had been dry, for a wet day would have meant having to pay for the cost of a hack so that his white stockings did not get spattered with mud.

Miss Grimes was a great believer in judging people by their friends, so she felt reassured that her decision to aid and abet Sir Charles had not been wrong when she first set eyes on Captain Tommy Hawkes. He was, she judged, only a few years younger than she was herself. He was a tall, ungainly man with powdered hair, bright blue eyes, a great beaky nose, a firm mouth, and a long chin.

He listened, amazed, as the plan of deception was outlined to him. 'Of course, if you've gone and told anyone about our marriage,' said Sir Charles, 'we'll need to forget about the whole thing.'

'No, didn't even tell Bohun, and I met him the other day. Don't socialize,' said Tommy ruefully. 'Not the sort of fellow who gets asked anywhere.'

'I am sure your association with the rich Sir Charles and the *very* rich Miss Page will bring you invitations to most houses,' said Miss Grimes.

'So,' said Tommy eagerly, 'how goes the plan of action?'

Miss Grimes picked up a sheaf of notes from a side table. 'I have not been out in the world for some time, but being the sponsor of a young heiress means I have something to sell, society being extremely cynical, or rather, *I* being extremely cynical about society. I wrote to a number of my old friends, now married, and bemoaned the fact that I felt myself unfit to do justice to bringing out a rich young lady. If I am not mistaken, I should start to receive calls by next week.'

Tommy's face fell. 'I would dearly love to stay and see the action, but I fear I must return soon to my regiment.'

Miss Grimes's experienced eye took in the well-brushed but old coat and the carefully painted shoes. 'We assumed you would be staying at Limmer's. Perhaps you would aid us by being part of this scheme?'

'I would dearly like to,' said Tommy awkwardly, 'but . . .'

'I have plenty of rooms here,' said Miss Grimes. 'You are welcome to stay.'

'Please do,' said Fanny. 'Charles would like it above all things, would you not, my dear?'

She put a hand on her husband's arm and he covered her hand with his own and smiled down at her. 'Oh, we must have Tommy,' he said.

Tommy threw Miss Grimes a startled look that she returned with an amused one. Sir Charles and Fanny looked the very picture of a happily married couple.

Dinner was a merry affair, Tommy, normally shy, feeling unusually at ease in such undemanding company. After dinner, they went back to the drawing room, where Fanny said she would play them something on the pianoforte, and Sir Charles stood beside her to turn the music.

'This is a rum do,' said Tommy in a low voice to Miss Grimes. 'What on earth does she want to go husband hunting for? She's perfect for Charles.'

'They will both find out very soon they are perfect for each other,' said Miss Grimes.

'I rely on your good sense,' replied Tommy warmly, and something stirred in the depths of Miss Grimes's lonely soul, a little stab of pure happiness.

She would not have been so happy had she known that her optimistic plans for Sir Charles and Fanny would go disastrously wrong.

51

*   *   *

At first it all seemed plain sailing. Society matrons called, invitations began to come in, news of the wealth of the 'cousins' spread through London like wildfire. The four plotted and planned in the evenings, played cribbage, dined, and talked, swapping stories about all the stratagems that were afoot to get the goodwill of this wealthy pair.

And then it was the day of their first social outing, Lord and Lady Varney's ball in Grosvenor Square. Fanny had very few qualms about going, for she would be escorted by Sir Charles, she would have Sir Charles to talk to and laugh with, and after the ball they would all gather in Miss Grimes's drawing room and exchange stories.

Both Sir Charles and Fanny were too involved in their own affairs to notice that Miss Grimes was subtly changing. Her severe face was more relaxed. Instead of hard starched muslin caps, she wore dainty lace ones. Her gown for the ball was of lilac silk shot with gold and of a modish cut. She wore a Turkish turban on her head of the same material.

Sir Charles had eyes only for Fanny. He thought she looked enchanting in a white silk gown with a silver gauze overdress and with silver flowers in her hair.

'You'll be the belle of the ball,' he said

proudly.

But Fanny was not.

She was dancing the cotillion with Sir Charles when she suddenly noticed his eyes fixed on someone who had just entered the ballroom—and that he colored slightly and his steps faltered. Curious, she looked to see what had caught his attention.

A beautiful girl stood there, surrounded by courtiers. She was as fair as Sir Charles, springy golden curly hair framed her enchanting face like an aureole. Her blue eyes were flirting this way and that as she received compliments from the men around her. She looked, despite her youth, sophisticated and at ease.

Fanny did not know that Sir Charles had recognized the beautiful face he had first seen in the miniature his mother had sent him. She also did not know that the beautiful Miss Woodward, for it was she, had been told by her parents of this rich Sir Charles Deveney and had been told to enchant him.

Fanny only knew that she felt suddenly insecure and lonely. The huge ballroom with its crystal chandeliers and its banks of hothouse flowers, its throng of bejeweled dancers, became an alien world in which she had no part.

And yet, because of the stories of her wealth, she was besieged by partners for the rest of the evening, and she laughed and flirted while her heart and feet began to ache. For Charles had danced twice with Miss Woodward—Fanny had discovered her name—and not once had he crossed to her side to ask her how she was getting on or to laugh or share any gossip.

'What is he playing at?' Miss Grimes asked Tommy Hawkes in alarm. 'This whole scheme is to find a beau for Fanny, although I did hope that they would realize the folly of it and settle down into being a happily married couple. Why is he making a cake of himself over Miss Woodward?'

'I recognize her,' said Tommy bleakly. 'You remember Charles told you that part of the way he was tricked into marriage was because the Pages sent him a miniature supposed to be of Fanny? Well, it was a miniature of Miss Woodward. He's been carrying it about with him. I've seen him looking at it. And now he's struck all of a heap. And only see the effect it is having on Fanny.'

When they returned home, a silent party, by common consent all went off to their respective rooms. Miss Grimes decided to have a severe talk with Sir Charles in the morning but was too depressed to tackle him that night.

Fanny went to her room and dismissed Miss Grimes's lady's maid, who was waiting up for her, and sat down in an armchair by the fire and stared bleakly into the flames.

The door opened and Sir Charles came

quietly in. He sat down on the floor at her feet and clasped his arms round his knees. 'I've found her at last,' he said simply.

'Have you?' asked Fanny in a small voice. She reached out a timid hand and stroked his fair hair; he almost absentmindedly reached up and took it and held it in a firm grip.

'Miss Woodward,' he said. 'Hers was the face in the miniature your parents sent me, Fanny. That face has been haunting me . . . and suddenly there she was. I—I am taking her driving tomorrow. I—I think I am in love, Fanny.'

'I am glad you have found someone,' said Fanny. 'Tell me more about her.'

He talked on while the flames in the fire sank down and Fanny held his hand tightly, wishing Miss Woodward at the devil.

'But I shall do nothing until you find someone first, Fanny,' he said, twisting round and looking up at her. 'What is the matter, my dear? You look so sad.'

'I suppose it is like losing a brother,' said Fanny on a little sigh. 'I have been so happy.'

'Fanny, I shall never leave you until this farce of a marriage is over. I am a beast to keep you up this late. You must go to bed.' He rose, drew her to her feet, and kissed her gently on the forehead.

'We are in this together, Fanny, this deception.'

'What will Miss Woodward say when she

finds you do not have any money?' asked Fanny.

'We will cross that bridge when we come to it.'

* * *

Sir Charles enjoyed a pleasant drive with Miss Woodward, blissfully unaware that behind him in the house in Grosvenor Square, three people had been praying for rain. But the sun shone and Miss Woodward was enchanting. Occasionally a deep chord of warning sounded somewhere inside him, a note of dread telling him that a difficult road lay ahead and that Fanny's happiness came first. But mostly he felt dizzy and elated. He was sure from the way she laughed at his sallies and looked up at him with her blue eyes that he had never been so witty or entertaining.

'Nice but dull,' Amanda Woodward said to her mother, sighing, when she arrived home. She untied the strings of her bonnet and tossed it petulantly into a corner.

'But so amiable, so rich,' said her mother.

'I thought *we* were rich enough.'

'*Tsk!* Only the vulgar talk about money,' said Mrs Woodward, a small, fussy matron, proceeding then to talk about it herself. 'The Woodwards have remained rich by marrying prudently. This is your second Season and you have already turned down several offers. You

56

cannot have another Season. People are already beginning to damn you as a sad flirt.'

Miss Woodward's eyes widened. 'Yes, you did not know that, did you? And the gentlemen close ranks sooner or later against any female they consider to be merely flirting with them. Sir Charles Deveney can only help your standing. He is considered the best prize this year, for the other candidates are either too old or too poor. There's Bohun, mind, but he has an unfortunate reputation. A sad crop this year,' commented Mrs Woodward gloomily—like a farmer looking at a bad harvest.

'You must try to befriend that little cousin of his,' she went on, 'and I will flatter that silly old woman, Martha Grimes.'

'What makes you think her silly?' asked Miss Woodward. 'She looks uncommon sharp to me.'

'Any woman who hasn't the wit to marry is stupid,' said Mrs Woodward roundly.

*　　　*　　　*

While Sir Charles had been driving Miss Woodward in the Park, Fanny had gone out for a walk. Miss Grimes had wanted to buy china in Pall Mall and Tommy had volunteered to accompany her. Fanny did not want to go with them. She wanted to walk by herself and think. She knew that if she had mentioned this plan,

Miss Grimes would have ordered a maid or footman to accompany her and Fanny wanted to be alone.

She walked through the streets of the West End, not noticing the goods displayed in the shop windows, immersed in sad thoughts of how she had been tricked into marriage, how she had at least found a friend in Sir Charles, and how life had become extremely complicated now that he was so obviously infatuated with Miss Woodward. If only *she* could meet that dashing black-haired man in the portrait, the man she had thought was Sir Charles. She became uncomfortably aware of the fact that well-dressed, pretty young ladies should not go walking alone in London, even in the West End, when one Bond Street lounger deliberately caught his spurs in her skirts and tore them, 'cracking the muslin,' as it was called. He cackled with laughter and she scurried off, her face flaming, and bumped into a tall, dark man.

She looked up at him, one swift, fleeting glance, and then stood stock still. Here was the man of the portrait. Above her, looking down at her quizzically, was the dark, ruthless, handsome face.

'Your servant, ma'am,' said Lord Bohun.

'I am sorry I bumped into you,' said Fanny, looking every bit as flustered as she felt. 'But some cad tore my skirts quite deliberately with his spurs and—and ... I suppose it is all my own fault for walking out alone.'

'Permit me to escort you,' said Lord Bohun. This charmer, he thought, might take his mind off Sir Charles Deveney. For he had just learned that morning that not only had Sir Charles come into a fortune but his cousin, a Miss Fanny Page, was a rich heiress and residing with him. He had hoped to escape from his own gnawing jealousy of Sir Charles by selling out of the army. But here was Sir Charles in London and the talk of society.

In an abstracted voice, he asked, 'What is your direction, Miss . . . er . . .?'

'Miss Page, Miss Fanny Page.'

'Bohun, at your service.'

He talked lightly of this and that as they walked along, while all the time his mind was racing. This then was Deveney's cousin. A beautiful little heiress. And from the admiration in those eyes—glancing up into his face from under the shadow of a pretty bonnet—his for the taking, if he put his mind to it. But if Deveney got wind of anything, he would soon put a stop to it. There had been that trouble with that Spanish woman. Only a Spaniard. No need for Deveney to cry rape, and all the while he chatted easily about plays and opera, while Fanny felt as if she were floating somewhere above the ground.

When they reached Miss Grimes's house, she looked up at him shyly. 'I am indebted to you. Is it Lord Bohun?'

He nodded. 'Lord Bohun. I shall never go walking on my own again.'

She summoned up courage. 'Would you care to step inside . . . for—for a glass of wine or a dish of tea?'

'Alas, I know your cousin, and I would rather you did not mention meeting me at all.'

Fanny looked at him in distress.

'But why not?'

'Various reasons I would rather not explain. I would not stoop to criticize the relative of so beautiful a lady. But we shall meet again.' His eyes seemed to glow as they held her own.

'I—I do hope so,' said Fanny breathlessly. 'I will not say a word to Charles, as you obviously do not wish it.'

'Do you go to the Marsdens' breakfast?'

'Yes, I believe so. Tomorrow, is it not?'

'I shall see you there.'

He raised her hand to his lips, deposited a burning kiss on the back of her glove, and strode off down the street. Fanny let out a little sigh of pure rapture and tripped indoors.

So that when Sir Charles returned, instead of finding a downcast Fanny, he found an elated young girl.

'You are looking very fine, Fanny,' he said, dropping a careless kiss on her cheek.

'I am feeling *very* well,' said Fanny. 'I think the air of London suits me. Are we going to the Marsdens' breakfast, Charles?'

'Aunt Martha has accepted for us. But to tell

the truth, my aunt has been out of the world for too long. The Marsdens are a most rackety couple and perhaps we should not go.'

Fanny's soft lips set in a stubborn line. 'I have never been to a breakfast before,' she said.

'There was our wedding breakfast.'

'That doesn't count,' said Fanny, sounding almost pettish.

'Fanny, these breakfast affairs, as you know, begin at three in the afternoon and can go on until dawn. Mostly they are served in the gardens, and if it should rain, everybody is bundled into the house in a sort of makeshift way.'

'It sounds like fun. Isn't Miss Woodward going to be there?'

'I do not know. I did say something about us going.'

'Then she will be there.'

'Why are you so sure, kitten? Is she enamored of my charms?'

'Of your fictitious moneybags, no doubt.'

'What a petty thing to say!'

'I am sorry,' said Fanny contritely. 'I do so want you to be happy—and will do nothing to stand in the way of that happiness. I mean, you would not stop me from enjoying the company of the man of my choice.'

'Of course not.'

'Swear. Swear on your heart.'

'How ferocious you are! There, I swear it,

61

Fanny. Whatever cavalier meets your fancy will receive a welcome from me.'

'Good,' said Fanny. 'I'll keep you to that promise.'

Lord Bohun made his way to the Chelsea home of the Marsdens. Mr Marsden was out, but his wife, Dolly Marsden, was pleased to receive him. They had had a brief affair on Lord Bohun's last leave. She was a plump little woman with china blue eyes and sandy hair. Sunlight struck through the window of her drawing room ... showing her appreciative guest that under her transparent muslin she wore nothing but stockings and garters. His senses quickened, but then he remembered Fanny.

'I want you to do something for me, Dolly.'

'Anything, my heart.'

'Have you heard of the latest heiress on the London scene? Fanny Page?'

'Of course. That is why I invited that old fright, Martha Grimes, to my breakfast. And what needs she do but demand an invitation for some army captain.'

'Name?'

'Tommy Hawkes.'

Lord Bohun's face darkened. 'Look, Dolly, I have an interest in this Miss Page.'

Dolly pouted. 'So you are bent on marriage after all?'

'Perhaps. But revenge interests me more. This Miss Page has a cousin, one Sir Charles

Deveney.'

'Yes, he is the reason that Miss Grimes and her dreary captain are invited as well. He stays with her. A delightful man I have heard. And *very* rich.'

'He is everything I despise, puritanical, straitlaced, always around to stop any fun and games. I would like to see him sweat a little.'

Dolly's face lightened. 'A game,' she cried, clapping her plump hands. 'What do you want me to do?'

'I want you to befriend Miss Page, to tell her that I am no end of a fine fellow, but subject to jealous spite from other army officers such as Deveney and Hawkes. You know me to be a brave man, desired by every lady in London, that sort of thing. Gradually introduce her to some of your ways and to that little gambling club you run.'

'You want me to corrupt her,' said Dolly.

He laughed. 'Did I say so? There's money in it if you play your part well. But nothing too obvious, mind. Place her next to me at your breakfast and put Deveney as far away as possible.'

'I heard a report that Deveney is much taken with Miss Woodward and her grasping mama is anxious to encourage him,' said Dolly. 'Mrs Woodward turned down my invitation but must have found out that Deveney was to be present, for she sent a note saying she had changed her mind, along with a giant box of sweetmeats. So I shall put La Woodward next to Deveney. Dear me, I never thought to be helping you in your love life, Bohun.' She glanced at him slyly. 'Here we are, all alone . . .'

He laughed and reached for her. 'One more time, hey, Dolly? No harm in one more time.'

CHAPTER FOUR

Martha Grimes carefully donned a new silk gown, one she had never worn before. It was pale lilac with a tucked and embroidered bodice, long sleeves, and several flounces at the hem. But the neckline was surely a trifle *low* for a lady of her advanced years. She tugged at it fretfully. But—she glanced out of the window—the day was very fine and warm, quite un-English weather. It would be hot in the Marsdens' garden, and therefore it was sensible not to be *too* covered up, and perhaps the captain might notice that she still had a fine neck . . .

She had to confess that her thoughts were now filled almost every minute of the day with thoughts of the captain. Yet she felt uneasily that time was flitting past and she had a serious situation on her hands. She had lectured Sir Charles about his interest in Miss Woodward, saying he should put all thoughts of his own happiness aside until Fanny was settled, but Sir Charles had listened to her gravely and had replied quietly that he was convinced that he could take care of his own future and that of Fanny's at the same time. Miss Woodward was all that was kind and beautiful. Once he had her confidence, he would tell her the truth and she would be a valuable friend for Fanny to have. Tommy had walked into the room at that moment and Miss Grimes had immediately, if temporarily, forgotten all about the troubles of this oddest of young married couples.

But she did reflect before they set out that Fanny had never looked prettier—or more enchanting—in a chip straw bonnet ornamented on the crown with marguerites and a filmy white muslin gown with a wide yellow silk sash. Her huge eyes sparkled and her perfectly shaped little mouth was pink and soft. Miss Grimes felt a slight qualm of uneasiness as she looked at that mouth. It looked ready for kisses. It was as if something had awoken Fanny to the world of men.

They made a merry, almost family party, on the journey to Chelsea. Sir Charles teased Fanny and said she was so beautiful his time would be taken up in fighting men off. Tommy told several very long jokes that he said had been told to him by a vicar, imitating the vicar's slow, lugubrious voice. The jokes were not very funny, but Tommy's delivery was. Miss Grimes laughed until the tears streamed

65

down her face.

But Miss Grimes became serious when their open carriage rolled to a stop in front of the Marsdens' home. She turned to Sir Charles. 'The Marsdens know some very *fast* people and Fanny is not used to such, so instead of romancing Miss Woodward and becoming *spoony* to the point of oblivion, you must watch over Fanny and see she does not get into bad company.'

Sir Charles smiled indulgently. He was very proud of Fanny. She had a freshness, daintiness, and charm unusual in the more jaded and painted beauties of London. But on arrival, they were asked to take their seats at the long tables in the garden and Sir Charles promptly forgot about Fanny, and everything else, in the delight at finding he was sitting next to Miss Woodward.

Captain Tommy was relieved to discover he was next to Miss Grimes. He was always conscious of the shabbiness of his clothes and his gaucherie in society. With Miss Grimes, he felt at ease and at home. He settled down to enjoy himself, making such an effort to keep her entertained that he succeeded for quite half the meal, until he saw Miss Grimes stiffen and her face grow set. 'What is the matter?' he asked quickly.

'Fanny,' said Miss Grimes. 'Who is that handsome man who is making her blush and simper?'

Tommy followed her gaze and his face darkened. 'That is Bohun,' he said. 'He was in our regiment and sold out just recently. An unsavory type.'

'And see how Captain Hawkes stares at me,' Lord Bohun was saying. 'And no doubt your cousin will be outraged when he discovers I am enchanted by you. Neither of them likes me.'

'Why?' asked Fanny.

Lord Bohun racked his brain for one of the least scandalous events in his life that had drawn the wrath of Sir Charles down on his head. 'It was in Spain,' he said. 'The time was boring, waiting for the French, and I was playing cards with two fellow officers and a Spaniard. I was winning, and the Spaniard suddenly upped and said I had been cheating. Deveney was called and examined the cards—and said in that cold way of his that the cards had been marked. Well, who do *you* think marked 'em? The Spaniard of course. But would Deveney listen? I was nearly court-martialed. He said there would be a hearing in the morning, but the Spaniard left during the night and left a note confessing that *he* had marked the cards.'

'So all was well?' ventured Fanny.

'Not a bit of it. Deveney needs must make a fuss and say that it was deuced odd that a chap who had marked the cards himself should start shouting about cheating. He said that the note was in good English. He accused me of either threatening the Spaniard or paying him to go away . . . and forging the note myself.'

'That does not sound at all like Charles,' said Fanny uneasily.

'Oh, that's very like Charles Deveney,' said Lord Bohun. 'He persecuted me so much that I decided to sell out.'

'It must all be a mistake,' said Fanny wretchedly. 'Let me speak to him.'

'No!' cried Lord Bohun. 'He would simply tell you more stories to discredit me. I do not blame him. He has had a hard life. His parents are wastrels, I believe. He envied me and my wealth. Now he is rich himself, he should not, but jealousy dies hard.'

The gentleman on Fanny's other side claimed her attention. She listened to him, apparently attentively, while all the while her mind was racing. She wanted to believe Lord Bohun, but how could she believe such things of Charles? The sun was beating down on the garden and she felt suffocated and had a desire to get away by herself, if only for a few moments. She deliberately spilled a little wine on her gown and let out an exclamation, then rose to her feet. 'How clumsy I am,' she said.

She tripped off in the direction of the house. Lord Bohun caught Dolly Marsden's eye and nodded briefly. She rose and followed Fanny into the house.

Dolly had been primed by Lord Bohun about what to say to spike Sir Charles

Deveney's guns.

'My dear!' said Dolly, catching up with Fanny. 'Is anything the matter?'

'I spilled a little wine on my gown,' said Fanny.

'Hardly a mark,' said Dolly. 'Fortunately it was white wine. Come to my boudoir and I will dab a little benzine on it for you.'

Fanny followed her plump hostess. Had Dolly been in one of her more outrageous gowns, then Fanny would have been wary of her. But Dolly was wearing a pretty sprigged muslin over a silk slip and looked like a motherly woman.

She fussed over Fanny and dabbed at the stain, finally saying, 'There you are. Not a mark.'

'You are very kind, Mrs Marsden.'

'Call me Dolly, and I shall call you Fanny.'

Fanny had no town bronze and assumed that ladies calling each other by their first names after a few minutes' chat was a London fashion. 'Don't go back yet,' Dolly went on. 'So hot in the garden, is it not? We shall stay here for a few moments and be cool. I am glad to see you are getting along famously with Bohun. Such a fine man! The catch of the Season. He seems enchanted with you, my dear.'

Fanny lowered her long eyelashes to hide her eyes and Dolly studied her shrewdly. 'Of course, that cousin of yours will not be pleased.'

'No?' said Fanny in a small voice.

'Alas, his jealousy of Bohun is legendary. His only fault, my dear. Do not look so miserable. But relatives can be so cruel. You must not let your cousin's jealousy stand in the way of your happiness.'

'I cannot believe this of Charles,' exclaimed Fanny. 'I *know* him. He is the kindest man in the world!'

'I am sure he is, Fanny. I am sure he is! But all men have a weakness . . . and your cousin's happens to be his jealousy of Lord Bohun. Now when Marsden was courting me, my brother tried everything to stop the marriage, and why? Because he thought no one good enough for me.'

'So what did you do?'

'I refused to discuss Marsden with him. I followed my heart and have never known a day's unhappiness since.'

Fanny reflected naively that love must indeed be blind, for Mr Marsden was an odd-looking fellow with a large head, and thick, wet lips, and a bulbous nose, but perhaps he had deteriorated rapidly in looks. Dolly saw her young guest was still not convinced and rose to her feet. 'London is a sadly rackety place,' she said, 'and full of *oddish* people. It is comforting to have a friend. If you ever want to call on me, I shall always be delighted to help and advise you.'

'Thank you,' said Fanny, extremely touched.

'Now, back we go, and do not listen to any nasty tales about Bohun ... because I can assure you he is the best of men and I have known him this age.'

So Fanny went back. She had been in the grip of a growing obsession about Lord Bohun ever since she had seen his portrait and was too inexperienced to tell the difference between love and obsession. As she approached him, she saw the sun striking down on his glossy black hair, and saw the strong, almost cruel lines of his face. He was tall and commanding, with broad shoulders and chest, a slim waist and hips. His very size, and his aura of strength, made her feel small and delicate and cherished.

Lord Bohun stood up at her arrival and smiled down into her eyes in a way that made her feel weak. It cost him an effort to produce that smile because the day was hot and the buckram wadding, which gave the width to his chest and shoulders, and the tight corset, which slimmed his waist, were making him uncomfortable and itchy. He wanted to go home and take off all these appurtenances of fashion, lie down in a cool room, and have a good scratch. But as he took Fanny's hand to assist her to her chair, he felt the way it trembled in his own and all his hunting instincts and desire for revenge of Sir Charles returned with such force that he forgot about his discomfort and settled down to charm the bewildered and dazed Fanny.

Miss Amanda Woodward fanned herself vigorously and with a little moue of irritation turned away from Sir Charles and began to talk to the man on her other side, an elderly gentleman who was quite startled to find himself the focus of the beauty's attention. Miss Woodward had enjoyed the first part of the meal, when Sir Charles had gazed at her rapturously. She had begun to revise her first opinions of him. He had a slim acrobat's body and very fine eyes. His thick, fair hair glinted in the sunlight. His hands were very fine, long and white, and well shaped. His voice was light and pleasing, with a slight husky note in it. And then his attention had suddenly become focused on his cousin and he had grown edgy and abstracted and had answered all her sallies mechanically.

From the top of the table, Dolly's shrewd eyes had noticed every little detail.

When the meal was at last over and the guests rose to walk in the gardens by the river, Sir Charles immediately went off in search of his 'cousin'. Miss Woodward stood for a few moments, irresolute. Sir Charles's sudden and seeming indifference toward her was something she was not used to at all and which heightened his attraction.

'Miss Woodward! Beautiful as ever.'

She became aware that Dolly was looking

up at her. 'Forget your admirers for a moment and walk with me a little,' said Dolly. 'There is a breeze from the river. Most refreshing. Such weather. The gods have smiled on my little breakfast. Sir Charles seems enormously taken with you, my dear.'

'He was, until he suddenly seemed to see something about his cousin that alarmed him,' said Miss Woodward, stabbing holes in the grass with the end of her parasol.

'Ah, well, she is an heiress and he is very possessive. The poor little thing is quite enchanted by Bohun—and Deveney hates Bohun—and men are so irrational, there is no talking to them. Deveney will try to stop his cousin from having anything to do with Bohun by filling her head with a lot of nasty army tales. Deveney is a fine man, a brave man, but he was always jealous of Bohun—regimental gossip, my dear—but if you wish to get that little cousin, Fanny, out of your hair, do, my dear, tell her not to listen to gossip about Bohun. I never gossip. So damaging. And if things were to go swimmingly with Miss Page and Bohun, then Sir Charles would be free to pay attention to more important things . . . like you.'

'But Bohun has a bad reputation,' pointed out Miss Woodward.

'La, the man was a rake, and weren't they all in their youth? No harm in that. Only look, there goes Sir Charles, he has caught up with poor Miss Page. And there joining them is that spinster, Grimes, and that odd army captain. Do, I pray you, put in a good word for Bohun with Fanny or they will have her a spinster for the rest of her days. Besides, as I said, Deveney should be concentrating on you.'

*   *   *

'You are my husband in name only,' Fanny was saying fiercely. 'And you gave me your solemn promise not to stand in the way of my happiness.'

'But the man is a cur,' said Tommy.

'And such a reputation, my dear,' put in Miss Grimes.

'I do not know what we are arguing about,' said Sir Charles. 'Fanny, you will do what you are told. You are not to see Bohun again or have anything to do with him.'

'Pooh! You are jealous of him.'

'You silly widgeon,' said Sir Charles, misunderstanding her. 'Why should I be jealous of Bohun when I am in love with Miss Woodward?'

Tears stood out in Fanny's eyes. 'It is you who are deliberately misunderstanding me,' she said. 'You all said you would help me to have a little fun, to enjoy myself, to find the man of my choice. *To find the man of my choice*, that's what you said. If—if you go on like this . . . well, we may as well end this farce and leave London—and be miserable together for the rest of our lives, Charles. I tell you plain, if you do not allow me to see Bohun, then I will tell everyone we are married . . . and—and poor. So there!'

'I could shake you!' Sir Charles glowered at her.

'Think on't,' said Fanny. She unfurled her parasol and walked off.

'Think you should have talked to her quietly,' said Tommy miserably. 'Little thing, Fanny, but lots of spirit. Hard to handle, but not a bolter or biter.'

'Not a horse, either, for heaven's sake,' snapped Sir Charles.

'We are all becoming overheated about nothing much,' said Miss Grimes calmly, although she felt far from calm. 'She has only just met the man. If he's such a black character, she will soon find out for herself. But so long as we stand in her way, and lecture her as if she is a child, and order her around, she will cling to him the more. She will be well chaperoned by me, Charles. There is no way she will be allowed to see Bohun on her own. Allow her infatuation to run its course.'

But if she does not find anyone decent, thought Charles, then I am indeed trapped in this marriage. But he sighed and said aloud, 'Perhaps. I will not criticize Bohun to her again. In fact, I must quickly reestablish our closeness, for that way she will tell me what that scoundrel is up to.'

So Fanny was left in peace to stroll with Lord Bohun in the gardens and to dance with him later, glad to see that Charles was once more engrossed with pretty Miss Woodward. Occasionally friends of the Marsdens would introduce themselves to Fanny and tell her what a fine man Lord Bohun was, how brave, how good, and Fanny would glow with pleasure.

Then there was the beautiful Miss Woodward, who kindly added her bit of praise for Lord Bohun. Fanny was a little disappointed to find her beloved Charles had such petty feelings, for she had begun to think him a saint, but he was only human, she told herself, and felt very old and wise.

Mr and Mrs Woodward invited Charles to their box at the opera the following evening, which he accepted, an acceptance that Dolly heard.

'So how goes the romance with Miss Page?' she asked Bohun. He was standing watching the dancers. Fanny was dancing with Tommy Hawkes, his clumsiness accentuating her grace.

'Very well,' he said. 'I shall now leave her to worry about me for a week, a week during which you, my heart, must see if you can find any weaknesses in her to indulge. I wonder if she gambles . . .?'

'Most ladies play cards.' Dolly looked up at him thoughtfully. 'I have one of my little parties tomorrow night,' she said, 'parties' being a euphemism for private gambling club. 'I overheard the Woodwards asking Deveney to the opera tomorrow night. I shall ask Fanny to come here and see if I can get her to agree to slip out without saying anything to the others. It might work both ways. I might be able to instil a love of the tables into her, and also relieve her of some of her fortune.'

'Do that. And see she drinks a lot. She sips at her wine like a bird and leaves most of it in the glass. I don't want to have a clearheaded heiress to pursue.'

Sir Charles had just finished waltzing with Miss Woodward. She curtsied and he bowed, then bent over her hand and kissed it. She gave his hand a brief little squeeze, a tiny little pressure, but it made his heart turn over. He put Fanny to the back of his mind. He wanted to live for the moment and not let the thought he was married and quite poor spoil anything.

Later, when he was to think about that evening, that beginning of all their troubles, he could only marvel at his own temporary insanity.

*   *   *

The journey home was silent. Fanny had a qualm of doubt about having accepted Dolly's invitation to meet 'just a few friends' on the morrow and 'no need to tell Deveney.'

Fanny had pointed out that as she had no carriage of her own—and could hardly ask Aunt Martha for the use of hers without betraying where she was going—there was no way she could keep her visit a secret.

Dolly had pooh-poohed that. She, Dolly, would send her own carriage, which would wait outside for Fanny at nine o'clock. Still, Fanny had been about to protest, but when Lord Bohun had smiled down at the lady with whom he was dancing, she had known raging jealousy for the first time in her life. And it was all Charles's fault that she had to be so secretive. Dolly had said Charles did not approve of her because she was a friend of Bohun's. It was too bad of Charles.

Sir Charles sat across from her and worried. Now that he was no longer in the magical presence of Miss Woodward, he was unable to live in the moment. He had overheard one of the ladies saying to another that Miss Page did not look *at all* like an heiress, as she had no jewelry to speak of.

He decided to ask Rundell & Bridge to send him a selection of their best jewels on approval. Then he would tell Fanny to wear the finest of them on their next social engagement—but to say loudly that she had quite made up her mind jewels were vulgar. There should be no half measures in tricking society. Suddenly a smile curved his lips as he again, in his imagination, felt that slight

78

pressure of Miss Woodward's hand; *She* would forgive him all. She was all that was sweetness and beauty. He had learned her first name was Amanda, and he murmured it soundlessly, over and over again.

Miss Grimes was wishing the pair of them at the devil. She and Tommy could have such a pleasant time if their days were not taken up in worrying what would happen when one or other of the young Deveneys decided to tell the truth. *Why did I ever agree to all this?* wondered Miss Grimes dismally. True, she would not have met Captain Tommy otherwise, but he would return to the wars and she would be left again, a lonely old spinster, and a spinster noted for being at the center of a scandal.

Charles went to Fanny's room that night, forgetting again Miss Grimes's lectures that he was not to be seen anywhere near her bedroom. Fanny was sitting at the toilet table dressed in a nightgown and lacy wrapper. She was brushing her hair with brisk strokes so that it shone in the candlelight.

'Oh, Charles,' she said bleakly, 'do not read me a jaw-me-dead. I have had enough this evening.'

The bench she was sitting on was long enough to accommodate two. He sat down beside her and stared at their reflections in the mirror, Fanny with her hair tumbled about her shoulders, he in a peacock blue silk banyan.

79

The oval mirror framed their reflected faces—Fanny and Charles—like a portrait of a married couple, he thought. But then they were married. There was a faint light scent of perfumed soap from the warm body next to his own.

'Dearest,' he said. 'I do not want to stand in your way. I gave you my promise. But Bohun is not for you. He is cruel and vicious.'

'Charles, everyone seems to know you are jealous of him, even Miss Woodward!'

'She never said so!'

'Yes, she did, Charles—and Dolly, too.'

'So it's Dolly, is it? She's a slut, Fanny.'

'I do not think I know you at all, Charles,' said Fanny in a voice that shook. 'I could be so happy—*we* could be so happy—if you would mind your own affairs.'

He sat in silence, thinking hard. Bohun had cleverly put about the gossip of his, Sir Charles's, jealousy. He would have to trust the goodness that was in Fanny to discover for herself the type of man Bohun really was. He and Miss Grimes and Tommy could keep a close watch on her. One thing was certain, she would never be allowed to see Bohun alone, and, therefore, any protests or complaints from him would only prolong her blind adoration of the man.

'I'm tired,' he said. 'I go to the opera with the Woodwards tomorrow. Oh, and I have decided to borrow some jewelry for you,

Fanny, so that you may look like the heiress you are supposed to be. You have nothing planned yourself for tomorrow?'

'I am making calls with Miss Grimes in the afternoon,' said Fanny, 'and then—and then I shall probably read in the evening.'

'Good night.' He stood up and bent forward, holding her gently by the shoulders and kissing her cheek.

He was no sooner out of the room than Fanny's vivid imagination replaced him with Lord Bohun. It was Lord Bohun who had taken her gently by the shoulders and given her that kiss. He had not said anything about seeing her again, but Dolly was his friend—and seeing Dolly was the next best thing.

*   *   *

True to his promise, Sir Charles presented Fanny with a dazzling array of jewelry sent 'for her approval' from Rundell & Bridge the following day. 'I think you can safely keep them for a couple of days, Fanny,' he said. 'We are going to Lady Denham's ball tomorrow evening, so you can wear some of the stuff then.'

Fanny turned over the brooches and necklaces, privately deciding to wear some of the best to Dolly's. But how was she going to escape from Miss Grimes? she thought, as she went on calls that afternoon.

She smiled at various hostesses and murmured inanities. These calls, Miss Grimes had said, were all important to 'nurse the ground', that was to get on the good side of London's most prominent hostesses, preferably those with marriageable sons.

Miss Grimes, who had discussed the matter long into the night with Tommy, had decided not to mention Lord Bohun's name.

'And so we will have a quiet evening without Charles,' said Miss Grimes when they arrived home again. 'Perhaps we could all play cards.'

Fanny bit her lip. It would be hard to escape from the house.

She thought long and hard about what to do, and then at dinner suggested that as it was a fine evening and Charles would not be with them, they could perhaps drive down to Westminster Bridge and look at the view. 'It would make a quiet change from racketing about,' said Miss Grimes. 'What do you think of that idea, Captain Hawkes?'

'Might be fun,' said Tommy lazily. 'Might take you ladies out in a boat.'

'I have never been in a boat before,' cried Fanny, clapping her hands with every evidence of delight.

It seemed all settled, but no sooner was the carriage at the door than Fanny suddenly pleaded a headache and said she simply had to lie down. Miss Grimes promptly exclaimed they would stay as well, but Fanny said it would only make her headache worse to think they had foregone such a pleasure as a sail in order to stay at home. She would ring for the servants if she needed anything. And with that, she practically shoved them out the door.

Miss Grimes and Tommy continued on their way. Soon the broad expanse of the river was spread out in front of them. Tke view from Westminster Bridge was very fine. On one side of the river were the groves and palace of the Primate of Lambeth; on the other side, the residence of the Parliamentary Speaker, under repair, and the huge bulk of Westminster Hall. The boats that plied the Thames were long, light, and sharp, and seemed to fly through the water. The banks of the river were not very ornamental. A few streets came down to it at right angles, but none ran parallel to the water.

Tommy hailed a waterman and asked him to ferry them along the river. The most handsome buildings, Miss Grimes decided, were in the long range of buildings called the Adelphi. Somerset House looked as if it might one day be magnificent, but as Tommy pointed out the work was going on so slowly that one half looked in danger of falling into ruin before the other half was finished.

Miss Grimes caught a glimpse of the gardens of the Temple, or Inns of Court, but mostly the view was generally dismal, the shores on either side choked with barges laden with coal.

At Blackfriars, the second of the three bridges that spanned the Thames, the view of a fine sweep of steps down the river was spoiled for Miss Grimes by the simply appalling smell. For here the common sewers of London discharged into the river.

'When you consider that all the filth of this metropolis is emptied into the river,' said Tommy cheerfully, while Miss Grimes held a scented handkerchief to her nose, 'it is perfectly astonishing that any of the people consent to drink it. One week's expenses of the last war with the French would have built an aqueduct from the Surrey hills and covered London in fountains. But there you are. We always seem to be fighting someone.'

Miss Grimes hung nervously to the side of the boat, for they were about to 'shoot' London Bridge. The passage under London Bridge was made precarious by the 'starlings,' or wooden platforms that protected the piers and created a swirling race under the bridge.

The boat lurched perilously and she was thrown against Tommy, who put an arm about her shoulders. She felt quite dizzy at the contact and was relieved—and at the same time lost and shaken—when he took his arm away.

Below the bridge, the bulk of the Tower of London cast its great shadow over the water. There were gloomy wharfs and warehouses on either side, and Tommy called to the boatman to take them ashore, where their carriage, which had followed them down the length of their sail, was to meet them.

As they stood waiting for Miss Grimes's coachman to arrive, she said suddenly, 'I am now uneasy about that headache of Fanny's. She is, I would judge, not normally given to lying, and when she talked about that headache, there was almost something *actressy* in her manner.'

'We'll soon be home,' said Tommy reassuringly. He sighed a little as he looked over the forest of masts in the river. The evening sun was golden. Everything swam in a hazy light, in the slight fog that hung about the corners of the streets of London even on the best of days. He felt so at ease with Martha Grimes, so far from war. He was war-weary, but unlike Bohun he could not afford to sell out. Like Miss Grimes, he often wished the irritating Deveneys would settle down to being comfortably married so that he and Charles could enjoy this rare holiday.

When they both finally alighted in Hanover Square, Miss Grimes said, 'I am sure Fanny will be lying down in her room. Where could she go? She does not really know anyone in London apart from us and cannot attend any social occasion unescorted.'

'Just go and see if she needs anything,' said Tommy, ever practical, 'and then we can have a comfortable game of cards.'

Miss Grimes went up to Fanny's room and pushed open the door.

The room was empty. Clothes were strewn all over the place—reminding Miss Grimes of days in her youth when she turned her wardrobe upside down looking for the prettiest gown. And the jewel box from Rundell & Bridge! It was lying open, and a quick examination informed the bewildered Miss Grimes that some of the best items were missing.

She ran downstairs to the drawing room, where Tommy was opening up the card table.

'Fanny! She's gone!' she cried. 'She tricked us. And she is wearing some of that jewelry.'

Tommy took her hands in his and said, 'Calmly now. Can it be Bohun? Bohun thinks she is an heiress, so I do not think he would queer his pitch by suggesting she meet him on the sly. Charles is at the opera. We will need to go there. Charles will know what to do.'

CHAPTER FIVE

Fanny enjoyed herself at first. All the ladies were so friendly. She had played faro before with her school-friends and remembered the excitement when one of the girls had managed to smuggle a pack of cards into the school. And just as she had lost a great deal of money

86

on paper to her school-friends, so it was here. 'We don't play for money,' said Dolly gaily. 'You just sign your vowels.'

So Fanny cheerfully signed IOUs in the comfortable belief that it was all pretend.

But as the evening wore on and the company began to drink more heavily, the conversation grew coarser. Fanny began to feel uneasy and wondered if Charles had in fact known what he was doing in warning her to stay clear of Dolly.

Just one more game and then she would go. She was playing against Dolly.

'And that,' said Dolly as she won again, 'means you owe me five thousand pounds.'

Fanny laughed. 'I shall just sign another of your intriguing pieces of paper and then I really must leave. Charles may be home himself soon and he will wonder where I am.'

And Miss Grimes, thought Fanny, with a qualm. She will already have found out I am missing, and what on earth shall I tell her?

'If you are going,' said Dolly, 'we should make arrangements. A draft on your bank will be sufficient.'

Fanny laughed merrily.

'If you do not have the necessary papers with you,' said Dolly, a note of steel creeping into her voice, 'do not worry, for I shall call on you tomorrow, or you can leave some of your pretty jewels.'

The glitter in Dolly's eyes should have told

Fanny that her hostess was quite drunk, for sober, Dolly would never have been so clumsy, but Fanny only felt lost and frightened. Five thousand pounds! Oh, they would need to run from London, and Charles would never see Miss Woodward again, and he would never forgive her, and she—she would never see Lord Bohun again, either.

As for the jewels! No, the scandal would be too much to bear if London society remembered them both for robbing its most famous jeweler.

Her nervous little fingers moved over the surface of the cards ... and then again. She felt infinitesimal little pricks on the smooth surface. She remembered a conversation Captain Tommy had had with Aunt Martha. He had been explaining the ways of card sharps. 'But how do they mark the cards?' Miss Grimes had asked. And Tommy had replied, 'Pin pricks.'

Her face hardened. Her mind raced. To call Dolly a cheat would not get her anywhere. The obsession about Lord Bohun left her body; her mind became clear and sharp and seemed to be working in double-quick time. As far as Dolly knew, she had been drinking heavily. But Fanny did not like strong drink, and, when Dolly had been concentrating on the game, had frequently decanted her glass into a hothouse plant next to the table. She looked around the room and saw the others for what they were—silly, greedy women obsessed with gambling. They were not friends of Dolly's. This was a gambling club and she, Fanny, was the gull, the flat, the pigeon for the plucking.

'I have decided to stay,' she said in a voice she made slurred. 'I have so much money, what is five thousand pounds to me?' My love, my life, my happiness, cried a voice inside her. But she went on aloud, 'But I swear these cards are unlucky for me. A fresh pack if you please, Dolly.'

Dolly's eyes gleamed with a hectic light. So the new pack would not be marked. But this little innocent, so well and truly foxed, would be no match for her.

And so they began to play again, but this time Fanny's mind was crystal clear. She was determined to play all night if necessary to cancel that debt.

*   *   *

Sir Charles stood impatiently outside the Woodwards' box at the opera, where he had been summoned by Tommy. 'Are you sure you cannot find her?' he declared impatiently. The opera ball followed the opera and he had dreamed of waltzing with Miss Woodward.

Tommy shook his head. 'I found Bohun at White's, gambling heavily, so she's not with him.'

'Dolly,' said Sir Charles heavily. 'That little

harlot thinks Fanny's an heiress—and I remember some fellow in our regiment telling how Dolly had gulled his wife by inviting her to a little party that turned out to be Dolly's private gambling club. Damn Fanny! I will need to make my apologies and go and rescue her. Oh, God, if she's lost a great deal there is no way we can stay in London . . . and I will be tied to that irritating featherbrain for the rest of my life.'

'No harm in her,' said Tommy awkwardly. 'Not up to all the rigs and rows of town. Needs a little bronze.'

'Pah,' said Sir Charles nastily. 'Wait here until I make my apologies.'

On the way to Chelsea, Tommy bravely tried to suggest to his friend that he forget about Miss Woodward and try to make a go of his marriage. Sir Charles did not even attempt to protest. Tommy's words did not seem to have any effect on him; his face was stern and set in the bobbing light of the carriage lamp.

'There she is,' said Tommy when they drove up outside the Marsdens' house.

The curtains at the bay window at the front of the house were drawn back. Dolly and Fanny sat at a card table in the bay. Sir Charles groaned inwardly when he saw the borrowed diamonds glittering around Fanny's neck and sparkling in her hair.

They entered the room just as a game was finishing. Sir Charles had expected a blushing and ashamed Fanny, but she looked up at him and said mildly, 'I am just leaving, Charles. How kind of you to come and bring me home. You owe me five hundred pounds, Dolly. A draft on your bank will suffice.'

Dolly looked at her in baffled fury. The shock of finding she had been outwitted by this innocent was sobering her rapidly—but doing nothing to improve her temper.

'I always pay my debts,' she said. She called a footman over and whispered to him. Fanny sat very still, her face hard and set, waiting.

The footman returned with a bundle of notes that Dolly passed to Fanny. Fanny counted them slowly and insultingly. At last she looked up. 'I prefer gold,' she said, 'but notes will do on this occasion.' She stood up. 'Your arm, Charles. Come, Captain Tommy. Miss Grimes will wonder what has become of me.'

Sir Charles waited until they were all seated in the carriage and then he shouted, 'What the devil do you think you were doing with that strumpet in that slap-bang shop she runs? You fool!'

'So I was a fool, but I repaired my losses,' said Fanny. 'I lost five thousand pounds because Dolly told me it was only pretend gambling and I believed her—until she started to demand a draft on my bank and suggested I leave some of the jewels with her. It was then I found the cards were marked and noticed that she was drunk. So I won back the money I lost, plus five hundred pounds, and I feel very clever. I am sorry you were dragged away from the opera, but you can go back now, Charles.'

'It is high time you realize the enormity of what you have done!' he raged.

But Fanny was triumphant. She felt she had just slain a monstrous dragon. She felt brave and clever.

'Why don't you shut your potato trap and give your tongue a holiday?' she said gleefully.

'You jade! How dare you speak to me thus?'

'Pooh! Because *I* am rich and *you* are poor.' And Fanny leaned back in the carriage and fanned herself with the bundle of notes.

'I shall talk to you later, when we are alone,' he said threateningly. 'You will never, hear me, *never* go anywhere again without my permission. I have a good mind to give you the beating you deserve.'

'I shall see you ride backward to Holborn Hill—with a book in one hand and a nosegay in t' other—before I let you lay a finger on me,' said Fanny, meaning she would see him hanged first. Fanny had enlarged her vocabulary immensely in just one evening.

Tommy tried to signal to his friend to stop berating Fanny because the more Charles went on, the more defiant and unrepentant Fanny became.

Miss Grimes was waiting for them when the carriage drew up. 'Why, Fanny,' she began, 'what . . .?'

But Fanny walked briskly past her and ran lightly up the stairs. It was left to Sir Charles and Tommy to explain what had happened.

'I will go to her,' said Miss Grimes, heading for the stairs.

'No.' Sir Charles put a hand on her arm. 'Fanny is my responsibility and I will deal with her.'

When he entered Fanny's room, she was carefully removing the jewels and putting them back in the box. She twisted round and glared at Sir Charles, then went back to rearranging the jewels.

'Fanny look at me!' he ordered.

Two small white shoulders raised in a shrug.

'I am not going to berate you,' he said sadly. 'You are young and untried . . . and were easily fooled by such as Dolly. No doubt, Bohun, who hates me, put her up to it.'

That brought her round, eyes flashing. 'You are going on like a real husband, Charles,' she said. 'Did I whine and complain about you going to the opera with the Woodwards?'

'Do not be such a widgeon. The opera with a respectable family and a gambling hell are worlds apart and you know it. What has happened to you? You are become so hard!'

Her face softened. With a little shock, he realized that despite her lack of inches, Fanny was very pretty indeed with her huge brown eyes looking almost black in the candlelight, her creamy skin, rioting black curls, and soft little mouth. 'I am in love, Charles,' she said simply. 'You know what it is like. Dislike of Bohun has colored your judgment. Look at the facts. He is very rich, so rich that my lack of money will not matter to him. What if I constantly complained about Miss Woodward, said she was only after your imagined money? Would that not hurt? Would you not deny it vehemently? Very well, I concede I should not have gone to Dolly's and I will not do so again—and I will be sharper when it comes to ladies of the ton who are not quite ladies.'

He studied her for a few moments, thinking hard. She had only really met Bohun at that breakfast. He had been very attentive to her and danced with her twice, but that did not amount to a proposal of marriage. Look at the courage and good sense she had shown in getting herself out of debt at Dolly's! Such courage and good sense would help her to assess Bohun's true character. By forbidding her to see Bohun, he would only give the horrible man all the added attraction of forbidden fruit.

'Very well, Fanny,' he said. 'I will not stand in your way, provided you do not get into any more scrapes.'

She ran to him and gave him a light kiss on the cheek. 'Oh, Charles, I knew you would see sense.'

Sense, his mind echoed as he walked back

downstairs to report to Tommy and Miss Grimes. Sense! Was he not himself as crazy as Fanny? Would such a prize as Miss Woodward not shrink from him when she learned that he was not only poor but married as well? Folly! And yet Miss Woodward—Amanda—had looked at him with such glowing eyes. He shook his head as if to clear it. Better not to think. Fanny was safe for the moment. Provided she told them in future where she was going and what she was doing, she could not possibly come to any harm.

*　　　*　　　*

'You owe me five hundred pounds,' Dolly was saying to Lord Bohun. Her guests had gone; she had sent them all packing as soon as Fanny had left and had then sent a footman to White's to summon Lord Bohun.

He eyed her coldly. She looked flushed and blowsy—and smelled abominably of stale brandy and perfume.

'Why should I?' he retorted. 'I did not tell you to cheat at cards. At least if you cheat at cards you should make sure you are not found out. It is better I distance myself from you from now on.'

Her eyes glittered with a hectic light. 'I would like to remind you again of that five hundred,' she said. 'You would not want me to tell your little heiress that it was you who put me up to inviting her, that it was you who circulated those tales of Deveney being jealous of you.'

He sat down at one of the gaming tables and swept aside the clutter of cards and dice and glasses with one savage movement. Dolly smiled and brought over inkwell, quill, and sand shaker. He wrote out a draft and handed it to her. Then he walked around the table and put his hands around her neck and squeezed hard, then shook her so that she gasped and choked.

'You say one word,' he whispered, 'and what you have just received will prove to be a foretaste of the real thing. You blackmail me and I will blackmail you. That husband of yours would not be so complacent were he to learn of our liaison. Ah, that has got you, has it not? The only thing that keeps you from whoring on the streets is Marsden, who lends you a certain spurious respectability. He goes along with your little schemes, for you make money for him. But hear this. Not only will I ruin your reputation . . . but I will damage you so badly that no man will want to look on you again.'

He released her; Dolly shrank back in her chair, her face white. He laughed. 'Hang me, Dolly, if you don't look as if you have just had a fright.' And still laughing, he thrust his bank papers in his pocket and strolled out.

Had Lord Bohun been a woman, he would most certainly have been excluded from Lady Denham's ball. Lady Denham was a high stickler, and, like the Countess Lieven, was fond of saying, 'It is not fashionable where I am not.' Any lady who had committed a whisper of an indiscretion was not allowed in her stately town house. But men were ever men, and everyone loved a rake. So Lord Bohun's dark past and dark reputation only lent him a certain added interest. Besides, he was rich and came from an old family. So he was invited, whereas a certain Miss Frampton, who was a model of good nature and courtesy, had been found to have had roots in trade and so was struck off the list and a chilly note sent to her—in which her ladyship frostily hoped that Miss Frampton would not have the temerity to attend.

Martha Grimes detested Lady Denham. They had been debutantes together in their youth. But Lady Denham always had the cream of society at her functions, and Miss Grimes was anxious to swallow her own pride in doing her very best for Fanny.

Lady Denham, having married a man considerably older than herself, was now a widow. She lived in a mansion during the Season in Grosvenor Square. She was a flat-figured woman, flat front and back, with an oddly squashed sort of face, like a face pressed against a window. Tommy whispered to Miss Grimes that Lady Denham looked like someone who had just been put through the mangle; Miss Grimes laughed, her clear, youthful laugh—one of her charms that was daily endearing her more to the army captain. Tommy would have been amazed and distressed to know that he was often the subject of the spinster's sad thoughts, thoughts in which she felt hopeless. He was only a few years younger than she, but she knew that although only in her forties, that was considered a great age—and that men in their forties were always attracted to younger women, never to respectable spinsters.

The ball was a very grand one. Fanny, looking radiant in a lilac silk gown cut low at the bosom and displaying the borrowed jewelry, was dancing with Lord Bohun, too naive to school her expression of absolute joy, thought Miss Grimes.

Lord Bohun had not had much opportunity to talk to Fanny because the dance was an intricate country one involving a lot of changing partners, but when they were promenading round the ballroom at the end of the dance, as was the custom, he said seriously, 'I am afraid I unwittingly introduced you to very bad company.'

Fanny's large eyes flew up to meet his. 'Mrs Marsden,' he went on. 'I believe she lured you to that gambling hell of hers by pretending to be a friend of mine.'

Fanny looked startled. 'But I thought . . .'

He shook his head. 'I have a certain affection for Marsden, but his wife is a sad rattle. Do not, I pray you, have anything to do with her again.'

'Oh, I won't!' said Fanny fervently. 'Charles was very angry with me.'

'Poor Miss Page. Ah . . . he has a vile temper.'

'Well, it was not like that, you know. Not at all. In fact, now I come to consider the matter, he could have been much angrier with me. I must be a sore trial to him.'

'He sometimes goes on more like a husband than a cousin,' said Lord Bohun, looking across the ballroom to where Sir Charles stood against a pillar, watching them steadily—and so missed the guilty blush that had risen to Fanny's cheeks.

'He knows I do not have any town bronze,' said Fanny quickly. 'But I am learning. Here is my next partner.'

'Are we never to be alone?' he asked, with such sudden intensity that Fanny felt her heart beat harder. 'We have another dance later. The waltz. We will talk then.'

Lord Bohun retired to a corner of the room and thought hard. To deflower Fanny would supply him with the perfect revenge on Sir Charles Deveney. She was an enchanting creature and an heiress. His pulses quickened as he looked across at her. He must plot and plan to get her on her own.

He began to get the glimmerings of an idea and went over to where the chaperons were seated and found a chair next to Miss Grimes. Tommy was absent, having gone to the card room. She went very stiff and haughty.

'I come to beg your permission to take Miss Page driving tomorrow afternoon,' said Lord Bohun.

Miss Grimes fanned herself vigorously. 'I think you should ask Sir Charles.'

He raised his eyebrows. 'Her cousin? Surely, ma'am, as her chaperon, you should say whom she sees or does not see.'

Miss Grimes bit her lip and wished Tommy were with her. Charles had said any obstacle to Bohun's courtship would only make Fanny want him the more. And where was Charles? Dancing with Miss Woodward—and certainly looking at that moment as if no other woman in the world mattered to him.

Fanny could not come to any harm driving with Lord Bohun in the Park. 'At the fashionable hour?' she asked cautiously.

'Of course.'

'Then I can see no harm in it,' said Miss Grimes, giving in with bad grace. That was men for you! Never around when you needed one, she thought, cursing the dancing Sir Charles and the absent Tommy Hawkes.

For his part, Sir Charles had just asked Miss Woodward to go driving with him the following day; she had accepted with such pretty grace that he forgot about Fanny, about being married to her. Miss Woodward was as tender and good as she was beautiful. She would be shocked when he told her about his marriage and lack of funds, but then those eyes would grow kind again and she would accept him. Like a number of army men, Sir Charles was singularly naive about women, and unlike most of his fellows, he had not taken prostitutes, having a healthy fear of syphilis.

Everything around appeared to disappear in a golden haze; Fanny, Lord Bohun, Miss Grimes, and Tommy—and even the hard, squashed face of his hostess. He had Miss Woodward floating round in his arms to the steps of the waltz and nothing else existed for him.

Even when Miss Grimes later told him that she had felt obliged to give Lord Bohun permission to take Fanny driving, Sir Charles only shrugged and said there was little that could happen to her in an open carriage and in the middle of a crowd of fashionables, and furthermore, he was going to be there himself with Miss Woodward.

'They are both quite mad,' Miss Grimes said, sighing, to Tommy, and then forgot her worries when he asked her to dance. He was a dreadful dancer, but Miss Grimes did not notice. She thought that she should forget any responsibility to Fanny and Sir Charles and concentrate on enjoying as much of Tommy's company as she could, while it lasted. She did not think much of herself, never had, and so the idea that he might propose, that they might have a future together, never entered her head.

Having all had a delightful evening, they were all in charity with one another on the road home, and, instead of going straight to bed on arrival, sat up over the tea tray, laughing and joking.

But underneath all their jollity was a darker strain of worry. Sir Charles hoped that Fanny would soon find out what sort of man Lord Bohun really was; Fanny was sure Miss Woodward was only interested in Sir Charles because she thought him rich; Tommy dreaded the day when he would have to return to his regiment and say good-bye to Martha Grimes; and Miss Grimes tried not to think of the bleak future without him and found it hard to do so.

*   *   *

Lord Bohun had been busy laying plans for the seduction of Fanny, but nothing but pleasure in her company showed on his saturnine face when he set off with her in a smart phaeton in the direction of Hyde Park the following afternoon. The fickle weather had turned cold and blustery after a sunny morning and Fanny, shivering in the thinnest of muslin gowns covered with an equally thin muslin pelisse, hung on to her bonnet and reflected that it was very hard to think love kept you warm when all the while you were worrying about watering eyes and a pink nose.

Fanny had not been schooled to flirt, but when they passed Sir Charles driving Miss Woodward—and so intent on the beauty that he did not even see his wife—a devil entered Fanny's soul. When they went round the ring again and she saw Sir Charles approaching once more, she began to flirt outrageously, casting languishing looks up at Lord Bohun, but having the satisfaction of seeing out of the corner of her eye that Charles had noticed her this time and was scowling quite dreadfully.

'I have to drive down to Richmond tomorrow,' said Lord Bohun, 'to see my old nurse. I would so like you to meet her. She is the only "family" I have left. She is very dear to me. She must be nearly eighty, a great age. Sarah Dunn is her name. Scotch. I say, would you like to meet her, too? There can be no harm in it if the day is fine and we take my phaeton. There is nothing in the unwritten rules of society that says a young lady cannot travel alone with a gentleman in an open carriage.'

Fanny's heart beat hard and she forgot about the irritatingly lovelorn Sir Charles. This was tantamount to a proposal of marriage!

'I would like that above all things,' she said. 'But there is the Bidfords' breakfast tomorrow and . . .'

'Sadie Bidford is a good friend of Dolly's,' he remarked.

'Oh!' Fanny's face cleared. 'In that case, I have every excuse not to go. I do hope Miss Grimes will not be difficult.'

'Let us return and ask her now,' he said gaily, privately thinking it would be easier to handle the spinster without Sir Charles around.

Tommy had gone out to meet some army friends and Miss Grimes, missing him quite dreadfully, although he had only been gone all of ten minutes, was in a vulnerable state and too obsessed with the missing captain to put up more than a token protest. Fanny, after all, was Charles's responsibility, and she had not known until Lord Bohun told her so that Sadie Bidford was a friend of the Marsdens. She weakly gave her permission.

Sir Charles had been invited back to the Woodwards to take tea—and by the time he returned, Captain Tommy had told the delighted Miss Grimes that an army friend had invited both of them to his box at the playhouse that night and rapture drove any thoughts of Fanny's future out of Miss Grimes's head.

Fanny thought it undiplomatic to tell her

husband her plans. Charles was nearly always cross with her these days. Let Miss Grimes tell him.

And so it was when Lord Bohun called to take Fanny out the following day that Sir Charles was in his room getting ready for the Bidfords' breakfast.

Tommy stepped forward. 'Bohun,' he said, 'just whereabouts in Richmond does this old nurse of yours live?'

'Peartree Cottage,' said Lord Bohun easily. 'It is just a little way along from the Star and Garter on the left. Old Miss Dunn will be enchanted to meet Miss Page. We will only stay for half an hour.'

'I don't like this much,' said Tommy after they had left. 'I am surprised Charles did not have more to say about it.'

Miss Grimes colored guiltily. 'I—I did not tell him. Oh, I meant to, I really meant to, but—but the visit to the playhouse drove it out of my head.'

'So Charles still thinks we are all going to the Bidfords?'

'As to that, Bohun said that Sadie Bidford was a friend of Dolly Marsden's and so it does to seem wise—'

'All ready?' asked Sir Charles, strolling into the room. 'Another fine day. We are having lucky weather. Where's Fanny?'

'She has gone to Richmond with Lord Bohun, to meet his old nurse.'

'What? Unchaperoned?'

'Well, Charles, he has an open carriage and—and it is in the middle of the day,' protested Miss Grimes, who had never heard of love in the afternoon.

'But we are expected at the Bidfords.'

'As to that, Lord Bohun did say that Sadie Bidford was a friend of Dolly Marsden and—'

'Fiddle! The Bidfords are friends of the Woodwards and all that is respectable. Where in Richmond?'

'He said Peartree Cottage, near the Star and Garter.'

Sir Charles's face grew bleak. 'You both must go to the Bidfords and make my humble apologies to Miss Woodward.'

'But Charles! Surely nothing can happen to Fanny!'

'But it is my duty to make sure it does not. Why on earth did no one tell me of this?'

Miss Grimes looked at him in dumb and guilty silence, for the correct reason was that they had all been so happy the night before she had not wanted to break the spell.

'Do you want the travelling carriage?' she asked after the silence seemed to have dragged on to an eternity.

'No, I will take my horse. Faster that way. Damn Fanny!'

With that, he strode out, leaving Miss Grimes and Tommy feeling like schoolchildren caught out in some misdemeanor.

CHAPTER SIX

Fanny, unaware of the turmoil she had left behind her, was enjoying herself immensely. This was one of her dreams come true, bowling out of London in a smart phaeton with a handsome man. As they left the cobbles at Hyde Park Corner and moved onto the gravel surface of the Great West Road at a smart pace, her heart sang. He had said this nurse was his only 'family.' That meant his intentions were serious and honorable.

Then a little cloud passed over the sun of her day. It was going to be terribly hard to tell him about that marriage. But perhaps she need not! How did one get an annulment? Did it take very long? It could perhaps be done quietly, with no one knowing about it. She was sure he loved her as much as she loved him. There was a new intensity in his gaze when he glanced down at her—and so in the brief burning looks that were mentally stripping her naked, Fanny read only the light of love.

Bohun could feel the weight of the cottage key in his pocket. He had collected it from his agent that morning. He owned many properties, his agent buying up places for him when they fell empty and renting them at a good price. Peartree Cottage at Richmond was a recent acquisition and not yet let to anyone. He had been to see it himself and knew it was perfect for his plans, those plans being the seduction of Fanny. He would pretend to be bewildered that the place was locked up, that there was no sign of his old nurse. Perhaps inside, *dear* Miss Page, there might be some evidence of what has happened to her. She may be ill. How fortunate that she gave me a spare key. And so his busy mind ran gleefully on. He was comfortably aware that Fanny was besotted with him. Seduction should not be too difficult.

When they reached the cottage, Fanny exclaimed in pleasure. It was low and thatched, with a riot of roses round the door and a neat, well-kept, pocket-sized garden at the front. Through the trees beside the house, she could see the lazy roll of the river, ruffled by a light breeze and sparkling in the sun. A few birds chirped lazily, a dog barked from the fields nearby, and there was the faint sound of music from somewhere, someone practising on the pianoforte, repeating the same phrase over and over again. And then, as they approached the low door, everything went absolutely still, not a sound. Fanny felt a qualm of unease but did not know why.

Lord Bohun hammered at the door with his fist; there was no knocker. Fanny waited expectantly for the shuffling of old feet on the other side of the door, but there was nothing but that eerie silence.

'Good heavens!' he exclaimed. 'I hope

nothing has befallen her.' He knocked again.

'Perhaps she is asleep,' suggested Fanny.

He took the key out of his pocket. 'Miss Dunn gave me this key,' he said. 'We should go inside and see if she is there.'

'I shall wait for you here,' replied Fanny.

'In truth, I would rather you came in with me,' he said earnestly. 'She may be ill, and I am not very good at coping with sick ladies.'

He unlocked the door and pushed it open. Fanny followed him into a neat parlor. She looked about. Everything was tidy and clean but had an oddly unlived-in air about it.

'Miss Dunn!' called Lord Bohun loudly.

Fanny listened to the echoes of his voice. What on earth would Miss Grimes say if she knew that she was alone in this cottage with Lord Bohun? thought Fanny. For she was all at once sure that there was no one at home. But Lord Bohun was making for the narrow wooden stairs that led off the back of the parlor.

'I had better see if she is resting.' He held out his hand. 'Come, Miss Page, I may need your assistance.'

Fanny hesitated. 'I think you should go upstairs by yourself, my lord. I will wait for you in that pretty garden. Should Miss Dunn be there and need my assistance, call me.'

Now the time had come to seize her in his arms. But she looked so small and dainty and trusting. Besides, he had left the front door standing wide open, and, as he looked, a couple strolled past arm in arm, talking loudly. So to perfect his plan, he would need to walk past her and slam that door, turn the key, and then proceed to ravish her.

Perhaps the best idea would be to let her go outside, to ascend the stairs, then call for her in an alarmed voice and get to work when he had her upstairs in the bedroom.

'I won't be long,' he said.

Fanny walked out and into the garden just as Sir Charles Deveney rode up and swung himself down from the saddle. 'Charles!' cried Fanny, running to meet him. 'What are you doing here?'

'I am come to save you from ruin. Where is Bohun?'

'He is upstairs, looking for his old nurse. He is afraid she might be ill. Really, Charles, you must stop following me around.'

'Look here, you idiot. I don't believe there is an old nurse or even was. Bohun's set on a seduction . . . and you are falling neatly into his trap.'

Lord Bohun had seen Sir Charles arrive from the upstairs window. Memories of Sir Charles's expertise at pistol shooting made him sweat in the confines of the small bedroom. He ran lightly down the stairs and let himself out through the back door. A solitary man was sculling past on the river. Lord Bohun hailed him, and when the man had rowed to the bottom of the garden and shipped his oars, Lord Bohun said urgently, 'Like to earn yourself a guinea?'

'So,' Sir Charles was saying, 'if you will just step aside, Fanny, I will go in there and give Bohun the beating he deserves.'

'Pooh!' said Fanny. 'You will only get hurt. He is bigger and stronger than you.'

She had backed to the cottage door and was now blocking it. He picked her up as if she weighed nothing at all and set her to one side—and walked in just as Lord Bohun was emerging from the back garden with a man behind him.

'Deveney!' exclaimed Lord Bohun with well-feigned surprise. 'What are . . .? No matter. This is a grave business. This person informs me that poor Miss Dunn departed this life last week.'

He took out a large handkerchief and covered his face and bowed his head.

'Oh, dear,' said Fanny in distress. 'How terribly sad.'

Sir Charles eyed the bearer of the sad tidings narrowly. The man was standing, twisting his cap in his large red hands and grinning sheepishly. 'How did she die?' he asked.

He noticed the way the man's eyes flew to Lord Bohun, as if for help. 'Dunno,' retorted the man, transferring his gaze to the blackened beams of the ceiling. 'Old age, I reckon.'

111

Lord Bohun uncovered his face. 'You have been of great help. I must be left alone now with my grief.'

The man tugged his forelock and escaped.

'We will be glad to leave you alone,' said Sir Charles in a chilly voice. 'Come, Fanny.'

'But you've only got one horse,' exclaimed Fanny, 'and poor Lord Bohun!'

'As you heard,' said Sir Charles grimly, 'he wants to be alone with his grief. Is that not so, Bohun?'

Lord Bohun, who had no intention of enduring further questioning from Sir Charles Deveney, sank artistically into a low chair and bowed his head.

Sir Charles took a firm grip of Fanny's upper arm and hustled her out.

'There is no need to be so rough. Or so unfeeling,' raged Fanny. 'That poor gentleman needs our help.'

'Don't argue. Up you get.'

Fanny gazed up at his tall hunter. 'But I am not dressed for riding, and you do not have a side saddle.'

'And I am not going to argue with you. You deserve an uncomfortable journey home.' He tossed her up into the saddle and then mounted in front of her.

'Hold on to me tightly,' he ordered. She put her arms around his waist as he spurred his horse away from the cottage.

After several miles of this headlong jolting,

Fanny shouted in his ear, 'Do stop, for goodness sake. I am feeling sick.'

He swung in under the arch of a pretty little inn, and when an ostler had seized the reins, he dismounted and then helped a white-faced Fanny down from the saddle. She staggered slightly when he released her and moaned, 'I do not think I shall have the proper use of my limbs again.'

The landlord came out to greet them and Sir Charles asked for lemonade to be served to them in the garden.

Soon Fanny gradually regained her color—and her temper.

'I am not a schoolgirl, Charles,' she snapped. 'I am quite able to handle my own affairs.'

He looked at her steadily. 'Do you know what I think, my sweeting? I do not think Bohun ever had an old nurse at that cottage. I think he bribed that idiot into saying he had the moment he saw me arrive.'

'Oh, you are determined to believe the worst of him!'

'All right. I will strike a bargain with you. If Bohun formally asks Aunt Martha leave to pay his addresses to you, if he places an announcement of your engagement in the newspapers, then you may do as you wish,' said Sir Charles, confident that such an event would never happen.

'I cannot let him print the announcement of

our engagement in the newspapers,' said Fanny. 'What if the vicar who married us should see it? Or any of the wedding guests?'

'Very well then. Let us forget about the announcement. If he is serious about you, then he will approach Miss Grimes in a formal way.'

'And if he does that, you will leave me alone?'

'On my honor.'

Fanny gave him a shrewd look. 'You are prepared to promise because you are easy in your mind that such a thing will never happen.'

He shrugged slightly. 'Drink your lemonade.'

The inn garden was very tranquil, with sunlight dappling the grass at their feet. The moving leaves on the trees above them cast flickering shadows over Sir Charles's face. What do I really know of him? wondered Fanny.

Aloud she said, 'What will Miss Woodward say to you going back to the wars?'

He smiled lazily. 'She will let me go. I can hardly use my wife's money to buy myself out.'

'What was your worst time . . . in the war, I mean?'

'Oh, that's easy. Corunna, or rather the retreat to it, stumbling over the mountains, men dying of exhaustion, women with babies dropping at my feet. The resentment of the men toward Sir James Moore was terrible to behold because he had ordered the retreat. "Why die in these awful mountains, running like dogs?" they said. "Let us turn and fight the French and die with honor." Discipline had crumbled. A great number of the soldiers were criminals released from prison to fight. Some of them I was happy to see die because of the misery they inflicted on the Spanish with their drunken looting and burning.'

'I thought the French behaved like that,' said Fanny in a small voice. 'Not the British.'

'It was the wine that started the problem. They were crazy for wine. In Benevente, the men found an extensive range of wine vaults under the square. The men fired their muskets at the casks hoping to puncture holes in them after they had dragged them up to the square. But the balls shattered the casks and wine gushed out in all directions until the street was ankle deep in it. The men tore off their caps, and, using them as ladles, drank from them. By morning the square was full of men and women so drunk they could not move, some still unconscious, with trickles of wine running from their noses and mouths.

'I was exhausted, too exhausted to care. I had been up all night protecting the home of an old Spanish lady. The men were mad to loot it, and how I kept them at bay I do not know, for they could easily have overrun me. The old lady thanked me with tears in her eyes. She was so very ill and frail. She gave me that old brass-bound chest that is with my luggage. "I can only live a few days," she said. "This contains my life, my memoirs. I wish you to translate what you find and make it into a book." I did not have the heart to refuse—and how I brought that ridiculous chest back over the mountains to the coast when most of the time I longed to tip it down a ravine is beyond me. But she had a certain quality of goodness, and she blessed me before I left, and I am sure her prayers brought me home.'

'It seems dreadful that women and children should be made to go on such a march,' exclaimed Fanny.

He sighed. 'You cannot stop them. After we arrived in Portugal, we tried to send most of them back. We said we would have a special ship to take them. But they would not go. I think that is what you call love, Fanny, and it makes our moonshine games seem a trifle ridiculous.'

Fanny folded her lips in a firm line. She would have followed Lord Bohun to the grave!

'But we heard tales that the Spaniards, the aristocrats, entertained the British officers,' she said, to try to lighten the atmosphere, for Sir Charles's face wore a haunted look.

He smiled suddenly. 'Evenings in Spanish houses were quite dreadful, Fanny. Large, sparsely furnished rooms, hardly any of them with a fireplace, and the men and women

116

facing one another across the room in long, formal rows. Card games, if there were any, were played in silence, and if there was music, you could hardly hear it because of the raucous hawking of the guests, both Spanish men and women spitting indiscriminately on the floor.

'Young women were hardly ever seen. Sometimes an officer such as myself, who was known to respect the strict rules of Spanish society, was allowed to dance with one of the young women at a private dance, but she was closely watched every minute. Refreshment was usually sugared biscuits and lemonade or cups of rich chocolate, or one of them would offer me the damp and chewed end of a communal cigar. A very proud and a very brave people, the Spanish, Fanny, but difficult for the average Englishman to understand.

'We ourselves were so proud and brave at the beginning as we marched along the banks of the Tagus with our drums tapping. It was autumn and the fields were flooded with hazy, golden sunshine, and, oh, the beautiful scent of wildflowers and shrubs: thyme, myrtle, sage and lavender, woodbine, strawberry and rockrose. Then we marched toward the Spanish frontier, through pine woods, and vineyards, and past convents and Moorish castles, like castles in a romance. But what a nightmare it all turned out to be.'

'You must dread going back,' said Fanny.

'No, my dear, it is my duty. This is the first

long leave I have ever been allowed. Besides, now we have Sir Arthur Wellesley as commander and he is a brilliant tactician.'

They fell into a comfortable silence until Sir Charles stretched and yawned. 'We must return or Miss Grimes will have people out looking for us—and I must change and go to the opera, present my apologies to Miss Woodward.'

Fanny looked at him doubtfully. 'You have been through so much, Charles. I would not see you hurt by this creature.'

'How dare you!' he cried, and their recent closeness splintered.

Fanny had the grace to blush. 'That slipped out, Charles! There is so much talk of our wealth. And—and . . . she is so very beautiful. But ladies will talk, and it is said she is a sad flirt.'

'Beauty such as Miss Woodward's always creates jealousy.'

'True,' said Fanny, downcast. 'We must not quarrel, Charles. Until our situation is resolved, we must be very, very kind to each other.'

'Then do not be unkind about Miss Woodward!'

'Nor you about Lord Bohun!'

'I'll try, Fanny.'

He rode back to London more slowly. Fanny, he wrapped tightly about him, was more worried about him than she had been before. It was not that she was in love with Charles, she told herself, but she did love him like a—like a brother. He was her Charles, and she didn't trust that Amanda Woodward one little bit!

*   *   *

Sir Charles turned over several suitable lies in his mind as he made his way to the opera that evening. He could hardly tell Miss Woodward the truth—that he was so sure Lord Bohun had meant to seduce Fanny he had run off to Richmond in pursuit of her. He wished the Woodwards had decided to stay on at the Bidfords' breakfast, where dancing would now have begun and where it would have been easier to hold a conversation, rather than at the back of an opera box.

As he made his way along the narrow corridor at the back of the boxes, he could hear the rising and falling of many voices, which showed that society found the production boring. No great diva or castrato was singing, and as society mostly came to the opera to see and be seen anyway, they were obviously enlivening the tedium of the evening in gossip.

He paused outside the door of the box and straightened his cravat and brushed at the sleeve of his coat with his hand. He needed new evening clothes. He had planned to order new clothes from Weston, the famous tailor, and then simply not pay him, but he found he could not do that. But his cravat was ornamented with a fine sapphire pin. Rundell & Bridge had been amazed when the 'wealthy' Sir Charles had sent back Fanny's jewels that morning saying they 'would not suit' and had sent him a present of the pin. Other tradesmen had lavished presents on him and on Fanny in the hope of getting the rich pair's custom. How to live on nothing a year, he thought wryly, and reached out to open the door of the box. And then Mrs Woodward's loud and carrying voice stopped him.

'You must show more warmth toward Deveney, Amanda. Goodness knows, you have flirted with enough men to know how to do it.'

Then came Amanda's voice, not sweet and charming as it was when she spoke to him, but high and shrill. 'I wonder if he is worth the effort, Mama.'

And then Mrs Woodward again: 'As you do not and have not shown any interest in any gentleman, you may as well settle for wealth.'

'I suppose so,' rejoined Miss Woodward petulantly. 'But it is all such a bore. Besides, I vow he is not really interested in me.'

'Then *make* him interested,' came Mrs Woodward's acid rejoinder.

Sir Charles stood stunned and bewildered, his hand to his heart. What a stupid dream he had been living in. All he had done was to make himself ridiculous and expose Fanny to the charms of Bohun.

He half turned to leave. And then he thought: No, I will play out this charade and get my revenge on the Woodwards. He opened the door of the box.

'Why, Sir Charles!' exclaimed Miss Woodward, her eyes flirting over her fan. 'You are come at last. And we are monstrous pleased to see you!'

*   *   *

Several hours later, Sir Charles made his way slowly home on foot. He had dismissed the coachman earlier. The streets were quiet and washed with moonlight. The watchman shambled past, calling the hour in a hoarse, wheezy voice. He had played his part well at the opera ball. He could see the nodding heads of the dowagers as they gossiped. He knew by his performance that he had been marked down as the beauty's future husband. And yet all he felt still was the sour taste of betrayal— and the knowledge that he was as much a fraud and a cheat as his parents, and deserved all of it.

He thought of Fanny's predicament with impatience. She would have to have her eyes opened to Bohun soon. If she wanted to find a real husband, she was wasting valuable time. Although he had been promised a long leave, he knew that the powers that be could easily and soon forget that promise and summon him back. And then what would become of pretty Fanny? She would either need to live in army quarters until his return or eventually rejoin her perfidious parents.

He crossed Hanover Square and let himself into the tall house. He climbed the stairs and walked toward his own room. He saw a light shining under the door of Fanny's room and pushed open the door. A branch of candles was burning brightly beside the bed and Fanny, propped up against the pillows, was reading a romance.

She looked up and cried, 'Oh, this is such a splendid story, Charles. I could not sleep until I had read some more. Goodness, look at the time! How did you fare? Are you forgiven?'

'Oh, yes.' He sat down heavily beside her on the bed.

She scanned his face. 'You look tired, dear, and . . . sad. Did anything go wrong?'

He shook his head. Why cause her worry about his miseries? 'I am concerned for you, Fanny. The whole reason for this mad escapade is to let you have some balls and parties and find the man of your choice. No! Do not bristle up. I shall not criticize Bohun. But I must point out that I have a feeling you will not bring him up to the mark. What will become of you if I am recalled?'

'I discussed that tonight with Miss Grimes,'

said Fanny cheerfully. 'She says that I can stay on in London as her companion.'

He had a sudden pang of sharp irritation as he looked at her carefree, glowing face. So no worries about the future for Fanny. He should have been glad, but he fought down a desire to shake her.

Instead he said, 'And what did you do? Did you and Miss Grimes go out?'

'No, we were very quiet and domesticated and played cards. Captain Tommy made us laugh so much. I think Miss Grimes is very fond of him.'

'Like a son?'

'Hardly, Charles. They are about the same age, are they not?'

'Don't start matchmaking, puss. Tommy is a confirmed old bachelor if ever there was one. Does London life suit you?'

'Oh, so very much. I am very happy, Charles.' She reached up, wound her arms around his neck, and gave him an affectionate kiss on the cheek. He could feel the swell of her breasts pressed against his arm and the faint scent of flower perfume from her hair.

'Good.' He gently disengaged himself. 'Get some sleep, Fanny, or you will never be fit for all the racketing around that Miss Grimes no doubt has in store for us.'

He rose and left the room. Silly Fanny, he thought as he finally stretched out in bed and prepared to sleep. But he lay with one hand gently across his cheek, as if protecting the mark of the kiss she had given him.

* * *

The following morning, Miss Grimes was thrown into a flurry by the arrival of a letter by hand from Lord Bohun. In it he said he wished to call on her that afternoon.

She flew to Charles's room and shook him awake. He read the letter with an impassive face and then said, 'It probably only means he wishes to ask your permission to take Fanny driving again. Make sure the expedition is no further than Hyde Park this time.'

'Oh, I shall! But this letter! Do you not think he wishes to pay his address to Fanny? And do you not think he is the kind of man to be quite furious when he finds out she is already married? I mean, he has only both your word for it that Fanny is still a virgin.' Miss Grimes blushed. 'She *is* still a virgin, is she not?'

'Of course,' said Sir Charles haughtily.

'It's just that . . . well, despite all my strictures, you do seem to run in and out of each other's bedrooms at all times of the night. Servants will talk, you know.'

'We are like brother and sister, I assure you. No need to worry about Bohun. He does not have marriage in mind.'

Feeling more at ease, Miss Grimes then

went along to Fanny's room to inform her sleepy charge that Bohun was to call that afternoon, no doubt to ask permission to take Fanny driving.

Captain Tommy, when he rose, also studied the letter but could not share his friend, Sir Charles's, optimism. 'The trouble is,' he said, shaking his head, 'that Charles hasn't seemed to have noticed that Fanny is a deuced pretty girl. But talk about not noticing what's right under your nose . . .'

'Exactly,' agreed Miss Grimes in a hollow voice. She felt like jumping up and down and shouting, *I* am under *your* nose!

She tried to calm her mind as the hour of Lord Bohun's arrival approached. Admittedly the man had an unsavory reputation, but then so had most unmarried men on the London scene. He was rich and he was titled—and he was probably genuinely in love with Fanny. She should not be so much against him, whatever Charles said.

'You'd best see him alone,' said Tommy. 'I can't bear the fellow, and I can't help letting it show.'

So capped and gowned like the most respectable of dowagers, Miss Grimes sat by the crackling fire, which had just been lit, for the day was cold, and waited for Lord Bohun.

When he actually arrived, she could feel her fears melting away. He was undoubtedly a very handsome man and dressed in Weston's finest tailoring, from his blue swallowtail coat to his glossy Hessian boots.

'Pray be seated, Lord Bohun,' said Miss Grimes, 'and tell me the reason for your call.'

'I wish to ask leave to pay my addresses to Miss Page.'

Although she realized she had been half expecting this while waiting for him to arrive, it still came as a shock to Miss Grimes. She studied him narrowly, but there was nothing in his eyes but a sort of anxious respect.

She found her voice. 'I do not need to ask you if you are in funds, Lord Bohun,' she said, 'so there is no question of your being unable to support Miss Page. On the other hand, you are an . . . er . . . experienced man and Fanny is very young and naive.'

'I am aware of that, madam. Miss Page will experience nothing more at my hands during our courtship than kindness and courtesy.'

'I should expect no less.' Rain clouds were gathering outside and the room grew suddenly dark. A log fell in the fire and a tall flame shot up, the red light shining on Lord Bohun's face, making his eyes glitter with a red light. Miss Grimes rang the bell and asked the servant to light the lamps and candles. The pair sat in silence until the room was illumined in a soft glow and the servant had retired.

'I think it would be better,' said Miss Grimes cautiously, 'if I gave you permission to court Fanny . . . but beg of you to leave any formal

126

engagement notice aside until you are both sure of your feelings and sure that you would suit. That is the best I can offer you at the moment.'

He bowed his dark head. 'You are most kind.'

'Very well.' She rang the bell again and asked the servant to send Miss Page in.

*   *   *

Fanny arrived so promptly that Miss Grimes was sure she must have been waiting on the landing outside the drawing room. She was dressed in a carriage gown of blue velvet with a naughty little hat like a man's high crowned one tipped rakishly sideways on her curls. Miss Grimes knew that Fanny's wardrobe had come from the hands of a village dressmaker, but that the girl had cleverly altered everything to a more modish line—so successfully, thought Miss Grimes, that it was a pity she did not decide to go into trade and set up in business. And that showed how low the spinster's thoughts had sunk, that she could even contemplate the idea of Fanny going into trade.

'My dear,' said Miss Grimes in a rather stifled voice, 'Lord Bohun has asked my permission to pay his addresses to you. I have given that permission—with the stipulation that no formal announcement of your

127

engagement should be made until you get to know each other a little better.' At this point, as Miss Grimes gloomily looked at Fanny's radiant face, she felt she should raise her hands and give the couple her blessing but found she could not.

'I shall leave you alone for a few moments.' She went out but left the door open.

Fanny smiled shyly at Lord Bohun. He took her hand and sank to one knee in front of her. There was an ominous creak from his corsets, but Fanny did not appear to have heard it. 'My heart,' he said, 'will you do me the honor of giving me this little hand in marriage?'

And just as Sir Charles walked into the room, Fanny smiled tenderly down at Lord Bohun's bent head and whispered, 'Yes . . . oh, yes.'

CHAPTER SEVEN

Lord Bohun rose to his feet but kept hold of Fanny's hand. 'Congratulate me, Deveney,' he said.

Sir Charles's eyes flew to meet Fanny's. 'Is this true?'

'Yes, it is true. And I am so very happy, Charles.'

Misery on misery, he thought bleakly. What could he say? Miss Grimes had obviously given

128

her permission. He could hardly protest, How dare you court my wife?

Lord Bohun's eyes held a mocking light. 'Well, Deveney, aren't you going to give us your blessing?'

'Not at the moment,' he said, and Fanny threw him a hurt and reproachful look. 'I will see how things go,' he added in a milder tone. 'We have never been friends, Bohun, so that is the best I can find to say at the moment.'

To Lord Bohun's intense irritation, Sir Charles crossed to the fireplace. He was obviously not going to be allowed any time alone with Fanny.

Then Miss Grimes came in, followed by Tommy. There was a long silence, during which Tommy, Miss Grimes, and Sir Charles surveyed Fanny and Lord Bohun.

'Perhaps Miss Page will come driving with me,' said Lord Bohun.

'But it is a dreadful day,' protested Miss Grimes.

'Not now. It's turned out splendid.'

And sure enough, the fickle English weather had changed again and pale sunlight flooded the room, bleaching the flames in the fireplace.

'There you are,' said Fanny tartly. 'The sun shines on our engagement, if you do not.' She tripped out of the room, followed by Lord Bohun.

Sir Charles sat down suddenly.

'I say,' said Tommy, 'I've been thinking.

Maybe Bohun ain't that bad. I mean, rape was never proved against him.'

'Rape!' screamed Miss Grimes.

'There was an incident with a Spanish woman,' Sir Charles said, sighing. 'She claimed that Bohun had raped her. I had the whole matter investigated. With drunken British soldiers raping nuns in convents, my fellow officers felt I was going too far in chasing Bohun. But on the day the woman was to report to me with her evidence, she disappeared. Several evil-looking louts from the village we were billeted in testified with amazing alacrity to the fact that the woman was a whore. I did not know much Spanish then; but I knew enough to be sure that they were lying. Other people in the village who had not come forward subsequently told me she was a respectable widow. But without the woman herself, there was nothing I could do.'

Miss Grimes was aghast. 'Did you tell Fanny this?'

'I could not, as nothing had been proved against Bohun. Therefore she has only my word against his, my unsubstantiated word. And would she believe me? Of course not. She dotes on the man. But she has not yet had time to get to know him. Let us pray she does, or I must seriously think about trying to stop this marriage.'

The butler entered. 'Mrs Woodward and Miss Woodward,' he announced.

130

'We are not at home,' said Sir Charles, without looking round.

'But Charles,' protested Miss Grimes, 'that is a most dreadful snub. Has anything happened?'

He collected himself with an obvious effort. 'This engagement of Fanny's has upset me. Show them up, Hoskins.'

Miss Grimes reflected sourly that Amanda Woodward was indeed a *shiner*. Her beauty lit up the room. Her manner and bearing were faultless. She smiled on Sir Charles with great sweetness. Miss Grimes noticed that although Charles smiled back and was very attentive to both Miss Woodward and her mother, he seemed to be acting a part. And all Mrs Woodward's hints that the day had turned fine and that Amanda was 'pining' for a drive in the Park appeared to fall on deaf ears.

She was relieved when the couple left. 'You were a trifle chilly, Charles,' she commented.

But Sir Charles was not going to betray that his infatuation for Amanda Woodward was at an end. He still felt ashamed that he had been so easily gulled.

*   *   *

'My heart,' Lord Bohun was saying, 'we should not inflict a long engagement on each other. So old-fashioned. I cannot believe you have come to love me.'

And guileless Fanny smiled up at him with her heart in her eyes and said, 'I loved you before I even met you.'

He laughed. 'How can that be?'

'You will find this hard to believe. I saw your portrait.'

'Which portrait? Where?'

'Sir Charles's parents have a portrait of you. I do not know how they came by it. You are on a charger on the battlefield. Most romantic.'

'I commissioned that portrait in Spain,' he said sharply, 'and shipped it home. But my agent informed me that it had been stolen by footpads.'

Fanny groaned inwardly. She had forgotten for the moment that her perfidious in-laws had pretended that the portrait was of Sir Charles.

'Actually,' she said quickly, 'it was not a portrait of you *at all*, but of someone entirely different, but so very like you all the same. Oh, do look. What a quiz of a bonnet!'

A less devious man would have pursued the subject, would have questioned her more closely about that painting, but he remembered in a flash all the peculiar stories he had heard about Deveney's parents. If he could prove they themselves had stolen his portrait, then that, by association, would discredit Sir Charles in Fanny's eyes. So he laughed and agreed the bonnet was quite dreadful and then talked of this and that.

'So we are to attend the Hardys' musicale

tomorrow evening,' said Fanny at last. 'Will you be there?'

'Alas, I must live without you for a few days. I have business on my estates to attend to,' said Lord Bohun. 'I shall think of you every moment I am away.'

As soon as he had bidden a fond farewell to her, he returned to his town house and found the preliminary sketches for that portrait, including a letter of agreement from the Spanish artist, and then sent his man out to find out where Sir Charles Deveney's home lay.

By morning, while Fanny still lay asleep, Lord Bohun was already thundering out on the Great Western Road in the direction of Oxfordshire.

*　　*　　*

He found that Sir Charles's home had been let to an American couple, a Mr Seaton and his wife, who were fortunately at home and pleased to receive him. He was glad he had not professed to be a friend of Squire Deveney's, for Mr Seaton began to complain almost immediately that he had been tricked, that the hall was neither as well appointed or grand as he had been led to believe in an exchange of letters, but that he and his wife had been billeted in an uncomfortable London hotel and too anxious for country air to look into the

133

matter as thoroughly as they should. The place was threadbare and the furniture shoddy, said Mr Seaton. It was furthermore ill-staffed and the tenants on the estates badly housed. It was all very well to say that as only a temporary occupant he should ignore such tiresome things as leaky roofs and high rents but he could not. He was an American and did not hold with people being treated like animals, raged Mr Seaton, the fact that he employed slave labor on his plantation in Virginia seeming not to count.

Having agreed with every word his host said—and having exercised his charm on the dumpy Mrs Seaton—Lord Bohun shook his head sadly and said he had worse to tell them. It was his belief that Squire Deveney was nothing more than a common thief. While they exclaimed in horror, he produced the sketches and the artist's letter, saying if they did not believe him, he would have the letter translated for them at his own expense, but that he believed Squire Deveney had come by a stolen portrait.

'I don't think I have seen anything like that here,' said Mr Seaton.

'Let me see.' His wife looked over his shoulder. 'I know that painting,' she exclaimed. 'It is in the attics.' She rang the bell, and, when a footman answered, said, 'Go up to the attics, John, the one with the broken furniture. You will find a painting, quite large, wrapped up in

134

a cloth just behind the door on the left-hand side.'

'There you are!' said Mr Seaton triumphantly. 'Now you can prosecute that rogue, Deveney, for holding stolen goods.'

'I am afraid I cannot,' said Lord Bohun. 'I am engaged to Sir Charles Deveney's cousin, Miss Page.'

'Any relation to the Pages of Delfton Hall?'

'Probably.'

'Must be another daughter,' said Mrs Seaton.

The portrait was carried in and unveiled. Lord Bohun looked at it with satisfaction. 'I am so pleased to have my property back. If you would be so good as to ask your man to put it in my carriage . . .'

He rose and bowed. He was making his way out when he suddenly stopped and stood stock still. He swung round. 'Why did you say about the Pages, it must be *another* daughter?'

'I heard talk in the village that Sir Charles Deveney, the son, that is—who, by the way, is highly regarded—married a Miss Page. But mind you, it is not an uncommon name.'

Lord Bohun smiled wolfishly. 'No, I am sure we must be thinking of some other family. Good day to you. Oh, by the way, your Pages, where do they live?'

'Over at Delfton Hall. You go to the crossroads and take the Banbury Road for three miles. You will see the gate posts topped

135

with griffins.'

'Thank you.' He bowed again.

He directed his coachman to Delfton Hall and then sat back, his mind racing. What was going on? Could it possibly be that the puritanical Sir Charles was actually tricking London society and passing Fanny off as his *cousin*?

He shook his head. Fanny was sweetness itself and would not be party to any deception. Still, it would do no harm to call at Delfton Hall.

Another shabby residence, he thought as his carriage swung round in front of the hall. The gardens, which consisted of shaggy lawns, had a neglected air.

A trim maid took his card and asked him to wait. She returned and ushered him through to a long saloon on the ground floor.

A gentleman rose at his entrance.

Lord Bohun strode forward. 'Mr Page?'

'The servant should have told you, my lord. I am Mr Robinson. I rent this place from the Pages.'

'Ah, but perhaps you can tell me about the family?'

'I cannot help you much there. You should ask the vicar. I did not actually meet them. My man of business arranged the rental of this house. We were anxious to move south from Northumberland, for my son is at Oxford University and I am afraid my wife dotes on

136

the boy and cannot bear to be too far from him. The house is neither as comfortable nor well staffed as my agent was led to believe, although there is an excellent cook. Of course, Mrs Friendly, the cook, will know about the Pages. Would you like to speak to her?'

'Thank you.'

Lord Bohun conversed amiably while waiting for the cook. He was feeling more confident now. He, who was so used to tricking people, could not believe he had been tricked himself.

Mrs Friendly entered the room. 'Ah, here you are,' said Mr Robinson. 'This is Lord Bohun, who has an interest in the Pages.'

The cook eyed the tall lord and did not like what she saw. Her usually open and cheerful face took on a shuttered look. She was loyal to the feckless Pages and had been used to the wiles of duns, who often had tried to masquerade as visitors in the past, although none had been so impertinent as to impersonate a lord.

'I have friends in London,' said Lord Bohun. 'Sir Charles Deveney and his cousin, Miss Fanny Page.'

Goodness, thought Mrs Friendly, what are they up to? 'The people who rent the Deveneys' place inform me that Sir Charles married a Miss Page . . . but yet he is courting a certain Miss Woodward in London—and Miss Fanny Page is affianced to me, so I find it hard to believe.'

What on earth are they doing? thought the anguished cook, but determined not to betray them. 'Yes, I believe the Deveneys and the Pages are related,' she said, amazed that her voice, not practiced in lying, should sound so calm and steady.

'So Sir Charles is *not* married?'

'Not as far as I know, my lord.'

He felt relieved—and at the same time disappointed—that the saintly Sir Charles was still on his pedestal.

'Thank you, Mrs Friendly. I was sure it was all a hum. You may congratulate me.'

'Why, my lord?'

'On my engagement to Miss Fanny.'

'Oh, to be sure. I do, my lord.'

'Splendid woman,' commented Mr Robinson when Mrs Friendly had left. 'The one good thing about this damp and shoddy place.'

Lord Bohun left, but when his carriage had reached the road he called on his coachman to stop. He sat there, biting his thumb. No! This was all wrong. There was definitely a bad smell about this! The *rich* Deveneys and the *rich* Pages? But what was it Mr Robinson had said? Ask the vicar. He called to his coachman to turn about and drive into the village and stop at the church.

The church door was open. He walked straight in, up to the altar, and turned left to

138

the vestry. There on a stand stood the large parish register secured by a chain. He opened it and began to read carefully through the births, marriages, and deaths without coming across either the name Page or Devency.

Again that feeling of relief mixed with disappointment.

'Can I help you, sir?'

Lord Bohun swung round and found himself looking at the gentle and rather sheeplike features of the Reverend Thwyte-Simpson. 'Miss Partington is taking tea with me,' said the vicar, 'and my maid told us she had just seen a gentleman entering the church.'

'I was looking through your register for a record of the marriage of friends of mine,' said Lord Bohun, now wishing he were on the way to London and feeling rather silly.

'I should be able to help you. Their names?'

'Sir Charles Deveney and Miss Fanny Page.'

He was so sure he would hear a denial that he half turned away.

'Ah, yes,' said Mr Thwyte-Simpson. 'Such a pretty wedding.'

'Could you show me the entry in the register?' Lord Bohun kept his voice low and even.

'Surely. Surely. Let me see. Yes, here is the christening of little Jimmy Wilkes, and before that . . . Well, bless my soul. Nothing here. And yet I stood by them when they both signed.'

'Let me see.' Lord Bohun almost elbowed

the vicar aside. He ran his hands over the pages and into the spine . . . and then he found it. He found a thin, sharp sliver of paper, all that was left after Sir Charles had cut the page out. But if he shouted that Deveney was a fraud, perhaps this vicar might even start to lie—as that cook had undoubtedly lied. Deveney, curse him, could command extraordinary loyalty.

'Dear me, yes,' he realized the vicar was saying, 'and Miss Partington was bridesmaid to Miss Fanny. A great day for her. Perhaps you would like to talk—?'

'Certainly,' interrupted Lord Bohun grimly. 'Lead me to her.'

The vicar looked at him rather doubtfully but said mildly, 'The vicarage is hard by the church.'

In the vicarage parlor, Lord Bohun bent over Miss Partington's hand. She blushed and simpered.

'Lord Bohun is a friend of Sir Charles and Lady Deveney's,' said the vicar. 'I told him that you were Lady Deveney's bridesmaid. Pray be seated, my lord, and I will ring for tea.'

'Such a wonderful day,' said Miss Partington, sighing. 'My gown was of white muslin. I thought I should freeze to death, but when I got to the church, I was so *elated* that I felt warm all over.'

'And Miss Fanny, how did she look?' asked Lord Bohun, still hardly able to believe it was his Fanny.

'Oh, like a fairy with that crop of glossy black curls and those big brown eyes. And Sir Charles just arrived from the wars. I was surprised to learn that the first time they set eyes on each other was on their wedding day— and even more surprised to be asked to be bridesmaid, for I had never been *intimate* with the Pages, Mrs Page damning me as poor genteel—when of course everyone knows the Pages to be as poor as church mice when they are not living on credit... and that goes for the Deveneys, too.' Miss Partington giggled. 'Aren't I naughty to gossip so?'

'But 'tis said that Miss Fanny is an heiress, and Sir Charles, too, has come into a fortune.'

'I know Miss Fanny is not an heiress, but did hear Sir Charles had come home with a great fortune in prize money.'

But there was no prize money, thought Lord Bohun. He had to get away and think. He refused the offer of tea, which had just been brought in, rudely and abruptly, and strode straight out without saying good-bye.

Once more he stopped his carriage on the road while he thought furiously. They were man and wife—but pretending not to be because they actually had no money. So they had hit on a plan. Fanny would marry the rich Lord Bohun and Deveney the rich Miss Woodward, and, provided they told no one about their marriage, they might get away with

141

bigamy. Damn them!

Then his eyes gleamed with a hellish light. He wanted Fanny. He had to admit to himself, he craved her. Now he had her where he wanted her. It was a pity Deveney had had her first. But no longer would he need to treat her like spun glass, and if she refused his advances, ah, then, all he had to do was threaten to betray her!

*   *   *

And yet, when he set eyes on her again, he found it almost impossible to believe she was cheating him. She looked so virginal, so glowing and adoring. He felt a wave of admiration for her. Few women could have played the role of innocent virgin so well. And he had only held her hand!

He was at a dance held on the lawns of Lord Anstey's Kensington mansion. Huge marquees had been erected, one for dancing, one for refreshments, and another for cards. Little colored lanterns had been slung through the trees and a full moon was riding high above. The weather had turned warm again, and the air was sweeter and fresher than that of London, perfumed as it was by the flowers and plants from the nearby nurseries that supplied produce to Covent Garden Market.

Fanny was wearing a delicate pink gown of filmy silk and had her glossy curls bound by a gold fillet, on loan from Miss Grimes. Sir Charles, he noted grimly, was still paying court to Miss Woodward but not looking over-happy about it. Perhaps, thought Lord Bohun cynically, that conscience of his was bothering him at last.

He entertained Fanny and Miss Grimes with several long and fictitious tales about the work he was doing on his estates, then courteously held out his arm and asked Fanny to promenade with him.

'I still can't like him,' said Miss Grimes to Tommy, who had just come up to join her.

'Oh, forget Deveney and Fanny,' said Tommy crossly. 'We spend too much time worrying about them and do not have enough time for ourselves. Let us go for a walk.'

She smiled up at him, then rose and looped her skirt over her arm and went out of the marquee with him and into the moon-washed gardens.

He held her arm in a comfortable grip. 'Not much fun being a soldier's wife,' said Tommy.

'Ah,' said Miss Grimes. 'You are thinking of Fanny.'

Here it comes, thought Tommy desperately. I can't go on like this. It's now or never. Into battle, 'cry God for Harry, England, and St. George.' I have faced the French *tiraillers* with less fear than I feel at this moment.

'No,' he said slowly and carefully. 'I was thinking of you. I was thinking of us.'

'But, Captain Tommy, you cannot mean . . .
Oh. I did not hear you right.'

'I am a poor soldier. I want to marry you.
But I have nothing to offer you but my heart.'

'Oh, Tommy, that is all I need.'

He crushed her to him and kissed her slowly
and tenderly on the lips.

'Now,' he said softly when he finally freed
his lips from hers, 'will you marry me?'

'Yes.'

'Oh, *dearest*!'

'And I will buy you out, as soon as possible,
so you need never go back to that awful war
again.'

He looked sadly down at her. 'It is not so
easy. I have a duty to do. The war cannot last
forever. Will you wait for me?'

'No,' said Miss Grimes. 'We will be married
by special license and I will go with you.' She
put a hand over his lips to silence his protest.

'But what of Charles? What of Fanny?'

'It is time this nonsense was over and they
solved their own problems,' said Miss Grimes.

'True. May I kiss you again?'

'As much as you want!'

*   *   *

Fanny walked under the moon with Lord
Bohun. She felt she had never been so happy.
For the moment, she had almost forgotten she
was married. When they had walked away

144

from the other guests and toward a part of the gardens shadowed by a huge yew hedge, Lord Bohun stopped and Fanny stopped, too, and looked up at him questioningly.

'This is the first time we have really been alone,' he said softly. He took her hand in his and raised it to his lips.

'We will soon have all our life together.' Fanny smiled up at him in the darkness. He seized her and kissed her full on the mouth, Fanny's first real kiss.

And she did not like it at all.

He was crushing her against him. He was kissing her so hard that she could feel her lips pressed back against her teeth. He smelled of brandy and cigars and sweat. He was mauling her mouth and his breathing was harsh and ragged.

With a great effort, she pulled free and said, with a nervous laugh, 'We are behaving disgracefully. What would Miss Grimes say?'

'A pox on Miss Grimes,' he growled. 'Come here!'

'I think it is not . . . it is not the . . . thing. Not now. We are not married.'

'No, we are not married,' he said.

But she was now too frightened and upset to hear him. 'I promised a dance to Charles,' she said, and turning, she fled from him.

He stood there, smiling. Let her play her pretty pretend-virginal games. He would soon have her—and there was nothing she could do about it.

Fanny saw Sir Charles walking with Miss Woodward. Miss Woodward was flirting very hard, eyes and fan going at a great rate, when Fanny came hurtling up.

'Oh, Charles,' she said breathlessly, 'we have a dance, I think.'

Miss Woodward looked furious, and Charles, amused. 'Why so we have. We will walk back to the ballroom with Miss Woodward, where I may turn her over to one of her clamoring suitors.' He offered Fanny one arm and Miss Woodward the other. He could suddenly sense Fanny's distress and wondered savagely what Bohun had been up to.

When Miss Woodward had been taken up by a partner, Sir Charles led Fanny onto the floor. It was a rowdy country dance, a lot of the guests having drunk too much and feeling that alfresco dancing allowed them to let down their hair more than they would have done in a formal ballroom. When they came together in the figure of the dance, Sir Charles noticed how Fanny's eyes roamed nervously about the marquee.

He decided he would find out what was ailing her when they promenaded after the dance. But no sooner had the music stopped than Miss Woodward came up to them, accompanied by her mother, and so he had no opportunity to talk privately to Fanny. But he

146

watched her for the rest of the evening, noticed that when Bohun claimed her for the waltz how she blushed miserably and hung almost limply in his arms, stumbling over the steps from time to time while Bohun looked down at her with a glittering air of triumph.

By the time they all climbed into the carriage to go home, Sir Charles was very worried indeed about Fanny. But Miss Grimes and Tommy announced their engagement and looked so blissfully happy that the journey home had to be taken up in congratulations and exclamations—and all Tommy and Miss Grimes wanted to talk about, over and over again, was how much in love they were and how neither of them had thought they had had any hope of attracting the affections of the other. So no future for Fanny, thought Sir Charles bleakly. Aunt Martha will no longer need a companion.

Fanny clutched the side of the carriage, her mind in a turmoil. What was it Mrs Friendly had said? That one got babies by kissing and cuddling! What if she were pregnant? All the elation that had coursed through her body every time she thought of Lord Bohun had fled. She had been in love with the painted man, the man in the portrait, and now reality had hit her like a hammer blow. She could appeal to Charles to take her away, but what of his love for Miss Woodward? Why should she destroy his hopes of happiness?

Back in Hanover Square, champagne was produced and the happy couple toasted. At last Fanny could not bear it any longer; she excused herself and went off to her room.

After some time, Sir Charles, too, said good night. He went to his room and tore off his cravat and coat and kicked off his shoes. Perhaps Fanny was not yet asleep. He must find out why she was so worried.

He opened the door of her room and walked in. She was sitting on the floor in a lacy nightdress and frilly wrapper, her bare feet stuck out in front of her, her head bent. She looked like a discarded doll.

He sat down beside her and put an arm about her shoulders—and she rested her head against him with a little sigh. He gave her a gentle shake. 'Out with it, Fanny. You've been looking worried to death ever since you went for that walk in the gardens with Bohun.'

Fanny gave a ragged little sigh. 'I think I am with child, Charles.'

He was too shocked to yell or remonstrate. 'How can you be?' he asked.

'Lord Bohun kissed me, kissed me very hard.'

'And?' He forced himself to wait patiently for the inevitable dreadful revelations.

'And he hugged me, like a—like a bear.'

'And what else?'

'I ran away.'

'Fanny,' he said in a wondering voice, 'there

148

must have been something else.'

'Isn't that enough?'

'No, my dear, not for babies.'

An anguished wail: 'But Mrs Friendly, our cook at Delfton Hall, she said that one got babies by kissing and cuddling!'

'Fanny!' He began to laugh, the relief was so great. 'You silly nincompoop! You have to do a lot more than that to get babies.'

She looked up at him. 'What, Charles?'

'I am sure Bohun will show you after you are married.'

'I would rather know now.'

'You had better get a lady to tell you. Miss Grimes.'

'You tell me!'

Still holding her, he bent his head and talked softly and earnestly, while Fanny looked at him, wide-eyed.

'Just like dogs in the street and beasts in the field,' she said at last. 'How ... *inelegant*!'

'Oh, Fanny, Fanny ... What a fright you gave me. What's in a kiss?'

'I didn't like it much,' said Fanny, 'but you see I have nothing to compare it with. Would you kiss me, Charles?'

'I have kissed you, my sweeting.'

'But just on the cheek. Kiss me on the mouth, here!' She pointed to her lips.

'Fanny, if the right man kisses you, there will be no question about whether you like it or not. Never say you have fallen out of love with

Bohun after promising to marry him!'

But Fanny stubbornly refused to even contemplate such an idea. She had held on to that dream for so long. Certainly it had faded during the Kensington party, but that was because she had been so afraid of becoming pregnant. She felt almost light-headed with relief.

'Oh, give me a kiss, Charles,' she said gaily. 'You have taken such a weight off my mind.'

He sighed. 'You are nothing more than a little schoolgirl, Fanny. Very well.'

He tilted her chin up and kissed her gently on the mouth. A sudden wave of sheer, unadulterated lust swept over him. These trusting lips were so soft and sweet. But one small, cold, disciplined part of his brain made him withdraw.

He cursed himself as he saw the dawning horror in Fanny's large eyes. 'I am sorry,' he said quickly. He got to his feet. 'It is a long time since I had a woman.'

He strode out.

Fanny sat on the floor where he had left her, her arms wound tightly about her body. That kiss had been wonderful, magical, beautiful. Like coming home. The horror in her eyes had been caused by the sudden realization that Bohun had been a fantasy and that she was already married to the man she loved. And he wanted only Miss Woodward.

A tear rolled down her small nose and

plopped into her lap. Well, he could have his precious Miss Woodward. For her part, she would tell Lord Bohun she had changed her mind. Then she would flirt and appear happy and carefree until Charles was settled. She owed him that.

CHAPTER EIGHT

During the following days, Lord Bohun wondered if he was ever going to have a chance to have a private conversation with Fanny. And how could he blackmail her into seduction if he could not see her alone?

The weather had changed to steady rain, canceling picnics and other alfresco events where he might have had a chance to lead her away from the crowd. He had tried to talk to her during a musicale and had been shushed violently. His vanity was so great that it did not occur to him that Fanny herself was making sure they were never alone.

But by the end of the week, blue skies stretched out somewhere far above the eternal smoky haze of London—and he was to escort Fanny to the Derings' barge on the River Thames, where the Derings and guests were to sail to Hampton Court. He called on Lady Dering a day before the outing and suggested to her that her guests would be sure to want to leave the boat at Hampton Court and admire the maze.

Sir Charles meanwhile was intent on playing his role of Miss Woodward's courtier so that Fanny should feel free to go ahead and marry Bohun if she wished, although he was still sure that she would soon find out what sort of man he was. Sir Charles had put the memory of that kiss firmly out of his mind. He had been overset; he had imagined his violent reaction to the touch of her mouth; all much better forgotten.

Miss Grimes had been made selfish by love. The only person who moved in her orbit was Captain Tommy, and if she thought at all about Fanny and Sir Charles it was with a sort of dismissive impatience. Let them get on with their own problems.

They were to meet Lord Bohun on the barge. As they were about to set out in Miss Grimes's carriage, Sir Charles took Fanny's hand to help her in, then started slightly at the current of emotion that seemed to be running between them. Fanny released her hand and nearly fell into the carriage, and then, as it was an open one, unfurled her parasol and dipped it to hide her face.

Captain Tommy and Miss Grimes were giggling and laughing like schoolchildren, so that the other two members of their party felt like striking them.

So indecorous at their age, thought Fanny

crossly.

'Tommy's making a cake of himself,' whispered Sir Charles, and Fanny nodded vigorously. Then she looked up at the blue sky hopefully—for the sign of just one cloud—but the day seemed set fair.

'Is Miss Woodward to be there?' she asked.

'Of course,' said Sir Charles bleakly.

'Poor Charles,' said Fanny, aware of his sad look. 'You must be very much in love with her.'

'I suppose I must,' he said. 'Let us talk of other things. Do you know the Green Man has finally gone completely mad?'

'I do not know anything at all about this Green Man.'

'Oh, his name is Haines and he was a famous sight at Brighton. He dressed in green pantaloons, green waistcoat, green frock coat, green cravat. He ate nothing but green fruit and vegetables, had his rooms painted green and furnished with a green sofa, green chairs, green tables, green bed, and green curtains. His gig, his livery, his portmanteau, his gloves, and his whip were all green. With a green silk handkerchief in his hand and a large watch chain with green seals fastened to the green buttons of his green waistcoat, he paraded every day on the Steyne, and in the libraries, erect like a statue, walking—or rather moving—as if to music, smiling and singing, as well contented with his own dear self as those around him, which made up quite a

153

considerable crowd, as you can imagine. He certainly had money, for his green food, including as it did choice fruit, sometimes cost him a guinea a day. He was seen at every place of amusement and entertained lavishly. But people did begin to get the idea the poor man was not quite right in his upperworks after he had thrown himself out of his windows several items and once over a cliff. So they locked him away.'

'That's sad,' said Fanny huffily. 'I like stories with *happy* endings.'

'But this one is true, you little goose.'

'Don't call me a little goose!'

'Why not? Only a goose would find such as Bohun attractive.'

'And what of Miss Woodward?' Fanny dipped her parasol and rolled her eyes in a parody of Miss Woodward flirting. 'Oh, Sir Charles. How strong you are!' mimicked Fanny. 'You actually managed to pick up that monstrous heavy handkerchief for me.'

'She is all that you are not,' said Sir Charles. 'She is womanly and graceful.'

'Oh, *thank you*. Thank you so much, dear Charles. Now I know what you really think of me. You are only jealous of Lord Bohun because he is taller and—and *stronger* than you are.'

'Fiddle and fustian. The man's a walking tailor's dummy. Where do you think his great chest comes from, hey? Buckram wadding.

And his waist? His slim waist? Corsets, Fanny. Still, he is an old-fashioned gentleman, I grant you that. Never got into this modern fad of washing properly, has he? Real eighteenth-century man. Just adds more scent.'

'And they call *women* cats!' exclaimed Fanny, her face flaming.

Both sat back in a sulky silence—and both then wondered why they were defending someone they had learned to dislike.

'I am truly sorry, Fanny,' said Sir Charles at last. 'I am peculiarly out of sorts.'

'Then I am sorry, too. We should not quarrel. We are in such a predicament. I say!' She leaned forward and whispered in his ear. 'Captain Tommy is a trifle bold, is he not? He has his hand on Miss Grimes's knee.' Her curls were tickling his cheek and he drew away sharply, as if he had been burned, and Fanny gave him a hurt look.

This is ridiculous, he thought. This is only my Fanny, who is like a sister to me. And at that moment they arrived at the Thames, before he could quite realize just how stupid that thought was.

On board the black-and-gold barge, Fanny was immediately joined by Lord Bohun. But Lord Bohun, to add spice to the coming blackmailing of Fanny into seduction, had decided it would be fun to woo her into a feeling of security. He apologized humbly for having treated her so roughly at the

Kensington party—and then set out to entertain her with mild gossip about London society and about the plays he had seen, until Fanny was quite in charity with him, and, although she could no longer look at him with the eyes of love, she decided he was proving to be such a friendly and sensible man, it would make her job of telling him that the engagement was at an end very easy after all. Having made up her mind to face up to the distasteful task, she was now eager to be alone with him, but for some reason, everywhere about the barge that they moved, Sir Charles and Miss Woodward were always there—and Fanny did not know that Miss Woodward was becoming more and more furious because Sir Charles seemed to be making a great point of avoiding being alone with her by dogging this 'cousin's' footsteps. And the setting should have been romantic: the orchestra playing, the waiters circulating with iced drinks and food, and the lazy river slipping past.

When they arrived at Hampton Court, the guests were first taken to see the famous vine, which was laden with grapes. It had nearly a thousand bunches and completely covered a hothouse of seventy-five feet long by twenty-five wide. In the far corner stood the brown twisted stem of the vine, almost lost to view, as if it did not belong to the magnificent canopy of leaves and fruit that owed their existence to it.

As they moved toward the palace, Lord Bohun fretted to find that Sir Charles's constant presence had been replaced by that of a tall German noble who appeared fascinated by Fanny and was entertaining her with his impressions of English society.

'The gentlemen are so rigid, Miss Page,' the German was explaining. 'I shall tell you a story, and you must believe that I speak only the truth. A lady of my acquaintance saw a man fall into the water and earnestly entreated the dandy who accompanied her—and who was a famously good swimmer—to save his life. Her friend raised his quizzing glass with the phlegm indispensible to a man of fashion, looked earnestly at the drowning man, whose head was just rising for the last time, and said, "It's impossible, madam. I was never introduced to that gentleman."'

Fanny laughed and exclaimed she did not believe a word of it, while Lord Bohun moved off in search of his hostess to make sure the guests would be taken to the maze.

They moved into the palace. Most of the rooms still had the same furniture as in the time of William III. The torn fabric of the chairs and curtains was carefully preserved. There were some very fine pictures to admire: Raphael's cartoons and two very fine portraits, one of Cardinal Wolsey and one of Henry VIII, his treacherous master.

Lord Bohun rejoined the party in time to

157

hear the German tell Fanny that he had stayed at Hampton Court the previous year and nearly died because his German servant, who had probably been too well entertained by some English colleague, had taken the burning coals out of the fire while he was asleep and left them standing in the middle of the room in a lacquered coal scuttle. 'The frightful smoke and infernal smell,' he said, 'fortunately awoke me just as I was dreaming that I was a courtier of Henry the Eighth and was paying my court to a French beauty at the Champ du Drap d'Or, otherwise I should have gone to meet the fair one of my dreams in heaven!'

Would the damned fellow never give over talking? thought Lord Bohun sourly. And why did Fanny have to appear so amused?

The German had moved on to discussing his bewilderment at English eating habits. 'After the soup is removed and the covers taken off, every man helps himself from the dish before him and then offers some of it to his neighbor. If he wishes anything else, he must ask across the table or send a servant for it—a very troublesome custom. Why do they not adopt the more convenient German fashion of sending the servants round with the dishes?

'And the intermediate dessert of cheese, butter, and raw celery is served with an ale so old and strong that if you throw it on the fire, it sets the place ablaze.'

'I am sure we English would find some

German customs very odd,' countered Fanny. 'You will not find spitting boxes in England.'

'Of course not,' said the German, with mock solemnity, 'An Englishman's spitting box is his stomach. No wonder they die young! And this fashion of "taking wine". You ask someone at the table to "take wine with you". Then you raise your glass, look fixedly at the one with whom you are drinking, bow your head, and then drink with the greatest gravity. Many of the customs of the South Sea Islanders are less ludicrous—'

'Miss Page,' interrupted Lord Bohun, with an edge to his voice, 'we are going out to the maze. Pray take my arm.'

'And pray take my other,' said the German.

'I am sure I am keeping you from the other ladies,' said Fanny, with regret. But she felt the moment had come when she should tell Lord Bohun that the engagement was over.

Lord Bohun had bribed the servant, who was usually placed on a stepladder above the maze to guide people out, to disappear as soon as he saw himself and Fanny moving toward the center.

They conversed amiably enough as they walked between the tall hedges toward the center, where there was a rustic bench. 'I have something to say to you,' said Fanny, 'and I had better say it very quickly, before anyone else joins us.'

'I do not think there is any fear of that.'

159

Lord Bohun looked up. Servant and stepladder had disappeared and there were cries of exasperation as the guests tried to find their own way out.

'Do not be angry with me,' pleaded Fanny. 'I cannot marry you. I am so very sorry. I am afraid we would not suit.'

He smiled at her. 'I have no intention of marrying you.'

'Oh!' Tears of relief started to fill Fanny's eyes. 'You are so good, so generous. I was afraid you would take it badly.'

'I think you misunderstood me, Lady Deveney. I do not need to marry you to get what I want.'

Fanny stared at him in disbelief.

'Yes, Lady Deveney. Your mistake was to tell me about that portrait of me. In my search for it, I was lucky enough to meet the vicar who married you. I gather the pair of you are still poor. Why you ever got married in the first place is beyond me, but the obvious plan seems to be that you each find rich partners. So unless you want me to ruin Deveney, you will do what I ask.'

'Where is that wretched guide?' came a man's voice from the other side of the hedge. 'I declare I will get the fellow horsewhipped when I find him.' And a female's voice answering, 'Oh, let us try this way.'

The voices faded. Fanny turned a white face to Lord Bohun.

'What do you want me to do?' she asked in a thin voice.

'Tomorrow you will meet me at the corner of the square, Hanover Square, and you will come away with me.'

'But I cannot leave with my baggage. I will be noticed.'

He laughed. 'You won't need baggage, my chuck. Besides, I shall take you up at nine in the morning. No self-respecting member of society will be awake by then.'

'And if I do not?'

'Then I will tell everyone that the Deveneys are married and don't have a feather to fly with. Deveney's reputation will stink to high heaven. I shall make sure that word of his deception gets back to his regiment. Of course, I shall tell the Woodwards before anyone else.'

'Charles was right about you,' said Fanny, her voice breaking. 'You *are* a monster.'

'You may call me any names you please. You have no alternative.' He reached for her as she shrank back on the seat. And then, with a little gasp of relief, she looked up and saw that the servant was back on his ladder.

She jumped to her feet and called out, 'Direct me out of here immediately, if you please.'

Sir Charles and a small group of people were waiting outside the maze. He saw Fanny's white face and strained eyes and took her aside.

161

'What has that bastard been up to?' he demanded fiercely.

'Nothing,' lied Fanny. 'We couldn't get out of the maze and I thought I was going to be trapped in there forever. Walk with me, Charles. Where is Miss Woodward?'

'Back at the barge.'

They walked silently to where the barge was moored. Sir Charles was immediately claimed by Miss Woodward. Lord Bohun came running up and joined Fanny.

'Pity Sir Charles had you first,' he murmured, and Fanny threw him a look of loathing, but no one saw that look.

On the way back, Fanny sat and listened to the orchestra and drank steadily, glass after glass of champagne. Lord Bohun left her to it. Let her drink and sulk all she wants, he thought. I have her at last!

Sir Charles sat down next to Fanny and said, 'Drinking a lot of that stuff, aren't you?' He gave a little sigh. 'Good idea,' and held up his glass to a passing waiter to be refilled.

The sun was sinking in the sky and turning the river to molten gold as the unhappy couple sat side by side and proceeded to get quite drunk.

Fanny's tipsy brain wrestled this way and that with the problem and found no way out, no way that would not damage Charles. Charles should not have kissed her so beautifully. But what was it he had said? That

162

it was a long time since he had had a woman?

Suddenly her brain seemed to become clear and sharp. Charles should have her first. Bohun thought he already had. Then let Charles have her for all his kindness and forbearance. He could use her 'unfaithfulness' with Bohun to get a divorce. He could have his Miss Woodward and live happily ever after. Had she not drunk so much, or had she been at all used to drinking heavily, she would have known better than to act on such an idea. She might even have realized that since that kiss she had fallen deeply and irrevocably in love with her husband. Sir Charles, wrapped up in his own misery, let the music slide in and out of his brain and matched his wife glass for glass.

'What a state you are both in!' exclaimed Miss Grimes as Fanny tried to step into the carriage when they arrived, missed her footing, and fell on her face on the carriage floor. Sir Charles tried to help her and fell on top of her.

'Bed for both of you when you get home,' said Captain Tommy severely. Fanny looked at him wide-eyed. 'How did you know?' she asked tipsily, but no one knew what she was talking about.

Miss Grimes remarked tartly that she never thought to see the pair of them 'come home glorious,' as the euphemism for dead drunk had it.

On arrival, she sent her maid to prepare Fanny for bed, confident that Fanny would quickly fall into a deep sleep and wake in the morning with the most terrible headache.

But although Fanny's legs were wobbly, everything in her brain still seemed crystal clear. When the maid had tucked her into bed, she murmured a well-manufactured, sleepy good night.

As soon as the maid had left and closed the door, Fanny got out of bed, fell on the floor, picked herself up, and sat in a chair and stared at the clock. She would give it fifteen minutes and then go to him.

The door opened and Sir Charles walked in. Fanny goggled at him. 'I was supposed to come to you. Lock the door, Charles.'

'Why? I only came to see if you were all right. We did drink rather a lot. Going to feel like hell in the morning, Fanny.'

'Lock the door!'

'Oh, very well.'

'Now come here and kiss me!'

'You are drunk.'

'Bohun's a beast.'

Sir Charles walked over and crouched down in front of her. 'So you've found out at last.'

She nodded solemnly. 'Now you can kiss me.'

'Oh, Fanny, Fanny . . . I'll kiss you for that. And then bed, promise?'

'I promise. That's the idea.'

He stood up, raised her to her feet, and kissed her gently on the mouth, but she wound her arms tightly about his neck and held him close. It was like the fireworks display in Vauxhall, he thought dizzily. Great golden stars were exploding in his head and deep, thick blackness.

They were both in their nightclothes, he could feel her breasts hardening against his chest, her nipples pushing through the thin cloth that separated their bodies. This is my wife, he thought with a sudden burst of gladness, and everything is as it should be.

He carried her to the bed, laid her down on top of the covers, and then lay alongside her and gathered her in his arms again, forcing himself to remember she was still a virgin, forcing himself to slow his pace, caressing her and kissing her until he knew at last she was ready for him. Had Fanny not been so drunk, the loss of her virginity might have been more painful, but passion and tenderness for her made Sir Charles a skillful lover. Naked, they moved gracefully in the dance of love, the one instinctively learning to pleasure the other, bodies writhing and turning and twisting, while the sounds of London life died away outside and the watchman's hoarse bark punctuated the hours.

They had gone to bed very early. Sir Charles, at last sated with love, fell into a dreamless sleep. But his now sober wife lay awake, knowing what she must do. Now that she loved him, it was more important than ever to protect Charles from ruin.

She dragged herself from the bed and slowly began to dress. She sat down at her writing table and wrote a letter to him—explaining why she had to go away with Lord Bohun and begging him to be happy with Miss Woodward. Then she unlocked the door, went to his room, searched until she had found his pistol, and put it into a capacious reticule. Then she went back and sat beside the bed, looking at her husband's sleeping face in the flickering flame of the rushlight in its pierced canister beside the bed. She slept fitfully in her chair, awakening with a start every now and then, her eyes flying to the clock.

Dawn filled the room with a grey light. Outside, the sparrows of London began to chatter awake. Then came the milk-maids calling, 'Milk-o,' and then one after another, the other cries of London: 'pies, mackerel, watercress, and strawberries.'

At five to nine, she rose and pulled a cloak about her shoulders. She leaned over the sleeping Sir Charles and kissed him on the mouth. He murmured and smiled in his sleep.

She placed the letter she had written on the pillow beside him. Then with one last look round, she left the room and went down the stairs. The clatter of dishes and the hum of voices rose from the servants' hall in the basement.

She unlocked the front door, grateful that

166

the lock was so well oiled that the turning of the large key hardly made a sound. She closed the door gently behind her and stood on the step.

It was a miserable grey morning and rain was beginning to fall. Over on the far corner of the square was a closed carriage, black with red leather curtains. Standing beside it was Lord Bohun.

With slow steps she walked across the square.

'Good morning, my love,' said Lord Bohun. He held open the door of the carriage. 'Get in.'

She hesitated with one foot on the step and cast an anguished look back at the house across the square. 'I can't,' she said suddenly.

He gave her a rough push on the back and sent her flying into the carriage. 'Hammersley,' he called to the coachman, before jumping in after Fanny and slamming the carriage door.

*　　　*　　　*

'It has been a long night,' said Mr Featherstone, stifling a yawn. 'Are we going to sit here forever?'

His latest love, Mrs Dolly Marsden, was seated beside him in his phaeton. He had set off to drive her home after a night of pleasure, but just outside the pillared portico of the church, just outside Hanover Square, she had given an exclamation and told him to stop.

Dolly watched avidly as Fanny walked slowly across the square, saw Bohun say something, saw Bohun thrust Fanny into his carriage, heard his voice clear across the square calling, 'Hammersley,' to his coachman. Had one glimpse of Fanny's white and anguished face at the carriage window as the coach rolled past.

'Now there's a thing,' said Dolly, paying no heed to her lover. She was still furious with Bohun over his threats. Hammersley was Bohun's country home in Gloucestershire. Elopements went to Gretna Green. Seductions, as Dolly knew too well, were often taken out into the country, as she herself had been some years ago, when Bohun had first had her. She was sure he was up to no good.

That spinster, Martha Grimes, lived in Hanover Square—and so did Sir Charles Deveney. Did Sir Charles know of it? She doubted it.

This was surely a way to get even at last with Bohun. She would tell Sir Charles what she knew and swear him to secrecy. *He* was an honorable man, unlike Bohun.

'Love of my life,' complained Mr Featherstone, 'I am getting deuced wet and so are you, or had you not noticed?'

Dolly jumped down from the carriage. 'I shall find my own way home,' she cried up to him.

'But what have I said? What have I done, my heart?'

Unheeding, she scurried off. The rain began to fall heavier than ever and Mr Featherstone realized, at last, that Weston's excellent tailoring was not immune to shrinkage and drove off.

Dolly hammered hard at the knocker on Martha Grimes's door. A correct butler answered it and stared disapprovingly at this wet matron with the highly rouged cheeks.

He was about to close the door in her face—without even asking her business—when Dolly shouted at him, 'Get Sir Charles and tell him his cousin has been abducted.'

The door swung wide and then the butler, forgetting his dignity for the only time in his life, ran up the stairs shouting, 'Help!' at the top of his voice.

Sir Charles was not in his room, so the butler flew to Fanny's and shook him awake.

For a few moments Sir Charles did not know where he was. All he knew was that he had a banging headache and this butler, Hoskins, was red in the face and yelling something at him.

At last he took in what was being shouted. Some person was downstairs saying Miss Page had been abducted. Sweet memories of the night collided with a wall of black fear. He leapt from bed and was about to rush to his own room to dress when he saw the letter on the other pillow. He snatched it up and read it feverishly.

'My dearest love,' Fanny had written. 'I must go with Bohun or he will betray us and you will never marry your Miss Woodward. Be happy with her. Do not think of me again. I will always be your Fanny.'

He crumpled the letter in his hand and then rushed to put on his clothes, after telling Hoskins to have his hunter brought round from the mews.

Miss Grimes appeared in her nightclothes, her nightcap askew. 'What's amiss?' she cried.

'Bohun's gone off with Fanny.'

'Tommy! I must rouse Captain Tommy!'

'No time,' said Sir Charles. 'Pray God I bring her safely home.'

*   *   *

Fanny's manufactured sleep in Lord Bohun's carriage soon became reality. He left her alone. He had no wish to start an undignified seduction in a rocking carriage. They would break their journey for the night at a posting inn in Henley-on-Thames. Perhaps, he mused, it might be better to leave her alone there, wait until he had her in his home. Yet why not take her? She could not cry out and alert the inn servants—or her precious husband would face ruin.

As the miles flew past, Fanny slowly came awake. She threw Lord Bohun a look, half scared, half defiant. He smiled at her slowly, and as she saw that smile, Fanny realized she could not go through with it. There was another way that Charles could be made safe—and that way lay in her reticule, in the form of one well-oiled and serviceable pistol.

She closed her eyes to fight down the wave of fear. She would need to kill him and then herself. She felt very young and lost. But slowly she began to experience a cold courage. If she had not been so light-headed and stupid, she would have accepted her marriage, have become a soldier's wife.

But it was no use worrying about what might have been. The rain was now falling steadily. The coach was moving more slowly now and lurching from one muddy hole in the road to another. A brief hope that the carriage might overturn and that Lord Bohun might break his neck flared up and quickly died. The time for dreams and fantasies was over. This was cold reality. She was about to commit murder.

By the time they reached the posting house at Henley-on-Thames, a deluge was falling. She stiffly got down from the carriage, ignoring Lord Bohun's offered hand, walked into the inn, and stood like a small statue while Lord Bohun ordered the best bedchamber for himself and his 'wife', as well as a private parlor.

When they reached the bedroom, there was something about Fanny's coldness and stillness that made him nervous. He needed to change

171

for dinner—but had no desire to expose himself in all his diminished form at this early stage when he took off his buckram-wadded coat. He told her curtly to get changed while he waited in the parlor.

'I did not bring a change of clothes,' said Fanny in a flat voice. 'I will wait for you.'

She walked off into the parlor without staying for his reply and shut the door behind her. Waiters were setting the table. She sat down in a chair by the fire after taking off her wet cloak and handing it to one of the servants, who took it off to the kitchens to be dried and pressed. She was wearing a plain serviceable gown. A wet feather on her hat was sagging down and tickling her nose. She untied the ribbons, took it off, and laid it on the floor beside her. Then she picked up her heavy reticule and held it on her lap.

She had had her moment in the sun, she thought bleakly. Hold on to that thought. Rain drummed against the windows with a monotonous sound. Laughter came from the corridor outside as a couple made their way out, laughter belonging to a sane world in which she no longer had any part to play. What a mad idea it had all been to pretend they were cousins. How stupid of them! But if Miss Woodward truly loved Charles, then she would marry him—and with his wife out of the way, Charles had no reason to tell her he had been married. She heaved a broken little sigh. All folly had its price, and she was about to pay dearly.

At last Lord Bohun came in, resplendent in evening dress. He scowled at Fanny's drab gown. Although he had said she would need no baggage, he had not expected her to come without even one change of clothes. He also felt that she might have tried to maintain the fiction of being his wife in front of the inn servants.

He walked to. the table and pulled out a chair for her. She rose stiffly and sat down without looking at him. He felt himself becoming more and more uneasy. Her face was white and her eyes made even more enormous by the violet shadows under them.

He ate a good meal while Fanny sat there like a stone, not touching a bite. She drank two glasses of water but refused any wine.

Lord Bohun had believed that once Fanny had become reconciled to her fate, she would behave in a ... well, more *womanly* manner. But the dignified little creature with the sad eyes, opposite him, had become peculiarly sexless.

When the covers had been cleared and the servants had retired, Lord Bohun grinned at Fanny, rose, and locked the door. Fanny slid the pistol out of her reticule, dropped the bag on the floor, and held the gun firmly on her lap.

'Now my beloved,' chided Lord Bohun, 'this

173

will not do at all. Accept your fate and be merry. Have some port. It will bring color to your cheeks.' He pushed the decanter toward her.

She raised the pistol, held it firmly in both hands, and pointed it directly at his heart.

He goggled at her.

'Put that thing away,' he shouted.

'No,' said Fanny, all deadly, frozen calm. 'I shall kill you first and then myself.'

He felt himself relax. She could never pull the trigger.

He stood up and walked toward her. 'Give me that,' he said, holding out his hand.

'Have it!' shouted Fanny, and pulled the trigger.

There was a miserable click and then silence. Then Fanny pulled the trigger again . . . and again . . . and again.

'It's not loaded!' cried Lord Bohun, and began to laugh.

Fanny hurled the pistol away from her, covered her face with her hands, and burst into tears.

'It is no use mawping and mowing,' he sneered. 'I would you were in a more . . . er . . . *loving* mood, but I shall have you here and now.'

Fanny took her hands away from her face and looked desperately around for a weapon. She had been so sure that pistol was primed. She should have taken the carving knife earlier in the evening.

But she was in a public inn, she thought,. and throwing back her head, she screamed, 'Help!' for all she was worth.

'Scream away,' said Lord Bohun. 'I told the servants my poor wife was given to manic outburts. No one will come.'

And then there was a deafening report of a gunshot. For one split second, he stared stupidly at Fanny, convinced that she had found another pistol, one that worked.

Then behind him, the door was thrust open and Sir Charles Deveney stood on the threshold, a smoking pistol in his hand. He had shot the lock.

Behind Sir Charles clustered a group of chattering and exclaiming servants.

'You cannot shoot me in front of these people,' snarled Lord Bohun.

'No, but I can thrash you,' said Sir Charles. 'Out into the yard with you, Bohun.'

'Don't,' whispered Fanny. 'Take me away, Charles.'

'Later. Out, Bohun.'

'But he will murder you,' cried Fanny, her eyes ranging wildly from her husband's slim, athletic figure to Lord Bohun's tall and broad one.

'Let him try.'

Bohun marched out past Sir Charles.

'Stay here, Fanny,' ordered Sir Charles.

But Fanny could not bear to wait and

175

wonder what was happening and followed him out and down the stairs. Cries of, 'A mill! A mill!' were sounding all over the inn.

The rain was drumming down on the slippery cobbles of the inn yard as Sir Charles and Lord Bohun began to strip to the waist, each handing his clothes to an eager gentleman who had volunteered to be second.

Despite her distress, Fanny could only marvel at how little there was left of Lord Bohun minus his splendid coat. The inn yard was crowded with spectators, and servants hung out of every window. More people were streaming from the town as the news spread like wildfire.

Lord Bohun was nearly insane with rage. The landlord, who had appointed himself referee, dropped the handkerchief and Lord Bohun flew at Sir Charles, his fists swinging. Sir Charles twisted and ducked, and then, with almost mocking ease, landed a punch full on Lord Bohun's aristocratic nose.

That was when Lord Bohun reeled back, and, reaching into his pocket, pulled out a dagger. Cries of 'Shame' rent the air. Several of the onlookers moved forward, then shrank back as the waving blade glittered menacingly in the light.

Lord Bohun and Sir Charles edged round each other, Sir Charles's eyes fixed on the dagger. His fair hair was plastered to his head like a helmet. The puckered scar on Sir

Charles's back gleamed lividly in the flickering lamps held by the spectators. Suddenly Sir Charles's foot lashed out and caught Lord Bohun on the wrist; the dagger went spinning across the cobbles. But that kick made him lose his footing and he fell on his back. Lord Bohun kicked him viciously in the stomach—and as Sir Charles doubled up, kicked him in the face.

Sir Charles staggered to his feet. Five men shouting, 'Foul!' held Lord Bohun at bay. Then as soon as Sir Charles had taken up his stance, Lord Bohun was released. Rage had given him new courage and energy. Sir Charles aimed his blows at Lord Bohun's head and body, but Bohun concentrated on the head alone. And then suddenly Sir Charles darted under Lord Bohun's guard and seized him round the waist with one hand, and, supporting himself with the other hand pressed on the cobbles, threw Lord Bohun clear across the inn yard with the force of a cross bullock. Lord Bohun's head hit the cobbles with a resounding *thwack*.

He lay still.

Men murmured congratulations and clapped Sir Charles on the shoulder, but there were no cheers. As one man said loudly; Bohun had fought as dirty a fight as he had ever seen.

Fanny threw herself on her husband's naked chest and he held her close. Rain and blood ran in rivulets down his face.

'Get me indoors, Fanny,' he said, with a shaky laugh, 'I shall look the deuce in the morning.'

He looked over Fanny's head and saw the landlord. 'Get Bohun out of this inn. Bring round his carriage and send him on his way. My wife and I will take his room.'

'Your wife?' exclaimed the landlord.

'My wife,' echoed Sir Charles, 'who was cruelly abducted by that bastard son of a whoremonger.'

Holding Fanny round the waist, he led her into the inn.

*   *   *

A surgeon attended to Sir Charles's face and said that apart from a few minor cuts and bruises, he would do very well.

'Now we really are a disgraced couple,' said Sir Charles as they sat by the fire in the parlor after the surgeon had left, Sir Charles in nightgown and dressing gown lent by one of the guests, Fanny wrapped in one of the buxom landlady's voluminous nightgowns. 'The local newspaper will carry a report of the fight and it will be in the London papers the day after tomorrow. If we were still the rich Deveneys, all would be forgiven. But society is not going to forgive a poor couple.'

'I don't care,' said Fanny. 'We are safe and
178

we are together, and that is all that matters. I still feel sick. I meant to kill, Bohun. I really did.'

'What a sad mess we have made of things,' he said. 'If we had just accepted our marriage, none of this scandal would have happened. But it is no use crying over the mess. We will drink our wine and eat some of that cold meat the landlord has left for us and go to bed. Tomorrow we will return to London and face Aunt Martha. You left your five hundred pounds. I brought it with me, so we can hire a carriage. Do you mind? Were you saving it for gew-gaws?'

'Anything of mine is yours, Charles,' said Fanny fiercely.

They sat down at the table and ate but talked little. Fanny was still feeling shocked and cold after the events of the evening and Sir Charles was suffering from an aching head.

At last, he stretched and yawned. 'Bed, I think, Fanny. We will cuddle up and keep warm—and leave romancing to another day.'

At first it was comforting to lie together, wrapped in each others' arms, but then Fanny began to feel hot and breathless and her treacherous body began to yearn for his. I am turning into a slut, she thought, alarmed. He must sleep. He must be exhausted. She disentangled herself and edged away from him.

His voice came to her ears in the darkness. 'What? No good night kiss, Fanny?'

She turned toward him and felt his mouth brush over her face, seeking her lips. And then a madness seized both of them as they kissed and kissed, and feverish hands removed nightclothes and sent them hurtling out of the bed.

When the first storm had passed and she lay, tired and drugged with lovemaking, he said softly, 'If it weren't for Aunt Martha, I would suggest we stay here in this bed for several days.'

Fanny gave a sleepy giggle. 'We are shameless.'

He raised himself on one elbow and looked down at her, her face glowing in the light from the fire.

'It's love, Fanny,' said Sir Charles. 'Only love.'

CHAPTER NINE

Miss Grimes seldom drank strong spirits and hardly ever gin. But as the news of the marriage of Sir Charles Deveney spread ahead of the couple's return to London, along with the scandal that they were not even rich, she felt she needed something to restore her nerves.

Ladies referred to gin as white wine; the dandies called it blue ruin; the laundress, Ould

Tom; the fiddler tossed off a quartern of max; the costermonger referred to it as a flash of lightning; and the Cyprian called for draughts of jacky. The linkboys and mud larks called it stark naked, while the out-and-outers added bitters to their gin and dubbed it fuller's earth. Gin was the comforter of both high and low, and on that sad day Miss Grimes refilled her glass from a squat bottle, too frightened to go out of doors and face the cold and contemptuous eyes of the ton. For she herself had been party to this deception. She and Captain Tommy were to be married the following week by special license. Miss Grimes had planned to invite a select few of the cream of society. Now she did not dare, for she knew all would refuse. Tommy had said staunchly that if they had never been embroiled in Sir Charles Deveney's affairs, then they would have never met, but on this grey London day, Miss Grimes found more comfort in gin than in her fiance's nobility.

The news that Deveney had boxed Bohun to a standstill had reached London on the wings of gossip as well. Bohun was disgraced, but not as badly as he might have been. The man was surely only taking revenge on the Deveneys for having tricked him and trying to get his money. His disgrace came from the fact that he had drawn a knife on Sir Charles and spoiled what might have been a good fight. Tommy was out gossiping with army friends to see if he could repair the damage. But she knew what they would be saying. Everyone would now remember all the conniving, cheating tricks of the Deveney and Page parents, and the talk would be of bad breeding and hereditary criminal tendencies.

What Miss Grimes had assessed of Sir Charles's character, however, did not tie in with that of a man who had seriously tricked Miss Woodward. It was all very well to point out that he was deeply in love with her and that the unmasking had been none of his own choosing, but still, now that the day of cold reason had dawned, there was no denying that on the face of it, he had played a sad deception on London's most prominent beauty.

Hoskins entered and said in a sepulchral voice, 'Mrs Woodward and Miss Woodward.'

'We are not at home,' said Miss Grimes sharply. Then she sighed. They deserved an audience, and the least she could do for Charles was to take the edge off any recriminations he would undoubtedly have to face from the Woodwards on his return. She held up a hand. 'No, Hoskins. I had better see them. Send them in.'

As she rose to meet them, Miss Grimes reflected that at least there were no signs that Amanda Woodward had been weeping. Her beautiful eyes were as hard as glass.

Without preamble, Mrs Woodward burst out into speech. 'I have a good mind to take the lot of you to court. It only surprises me that the duns are not on your doorstep.'

'No bills are owed by anyone in this house,' said Miss Grimes, edging the gin bottle further under her chair with her foot. 'Pray be seated.'

'You must have been party to this deception,' said Miss Woodward in a thin voice.

Miss Grimes opened her mouth to explain that the Deveneys had been kicked into marriage, that Sir Charles's intentions toward Miss Woodward had been honorable, that he had intended to get an annulment, but she quickly realized that such explanations would only add fuel to the fire.

'My heart has been shattered,' went on Miss Woodward, taking out a lace handkerchief and dabbing carefully, first at one dry eye and then at the other.

'Then you know at last how it feels,' said Miss Grimes tartly. 'And it may stop you from playing fast and loose with the affections of other gentlemen.'

'How dare you?' exclaimed Mrs Woodward. 'My daughter's tenderest affections have been blighted. Her heart is broken. Dr. Markenzie fears she may go into a decline.'

Miss Woodward immediately struck an Attitude. She put one limp hand to her brow and stretched the other out in front of her, as if warding off further humiliations, and threw her head back and stared at the ceiling.

That was when Sir Charles Deveney and Fanny walked into the room. Miss Woodward screamed and fell to the floor in a faint, or rather in a well-manufactured faint. Her mother stooped over her, crying, 'Fetch the constable! Fetch the watch! Fetch the militia! Have these murderers locked up!'

'Fiddlesticks,' said Sir Charles wearily. He escorted Fanny to a chair and then sat down himself—and studied the distressed tableau with indifferent eyes. Miss Woodward promptly sat up, the healthy pink in her cheeks giving the lie to her 'faint'.

'What did you say?' she demanded menacingly.

Mrs Woodward helped her daughter into a chair.

'I will repeat a conversation between you and your daughter,' said Sir Charles, 'that I overheard when I was about to join you in your box at the opera. You, Mrs Woodward said, "You must show more warmth toward Deveney, Amanda. Goodness knows, you have flirted with enough men to know how to do it." To which you, Miss Woodward, replied, "I wonder if he is worth the effort, Mama," Mrs Woodward rejoined, "As you do not and have not shown any interest in any gentleman, you may as well settle for wealth." And the beautiful Miss Woodward replied, "But it is all such a bore." Do not question the accuracy of my report. The words were burned into my

184

soul. Had it not been that your only interest in me was because of my supposed money, then I would feel shame. As it is, I think you have learned a good lesson.'

Miss Woodward rose to her feet, her face flaming. 'Take me away from these persons, Mama.' She stamped her foot. 'You should never have brought me here.'

Sir Charles, Fanny, and Miss Grimes sat in silence as they hurried out.

'So you see the damage you have done?' cried Miss Grimes. 'Oh, she deserved her comeuppance, I grant you. But did I? I am shamed by being party to your behavior. I am marrying Captain Tommy next week by special license, and no one will come to the wedding because of the disgrace.'

'Oh, Miss Grimes,' said Fanny, tears starting to fill her eyes. 'Charles and I are so happy now. We are *glad* we are married to each other.'

'What?' screeched the outraged Miss Grimes. 'Oh, that's very fine. So we all went through all this for nothing! If the pair of you had the brains you were born with, you would have realized a long time ago that you were made for each other.'

'We are leaving,' said Sir Charles. 'You will not have to bear the burden of our company any longer.'

'But where will you go?'

'We shall return to barracks and married

quarters will be found for us. Come Fanny. I apologize to you, Aunt Martha, from the bottom of my heart. Fanny and I have been very silly, but you will be plagued with us no longer.'

They walked out together, and Miss Grimes scrabbled under her chair for the gin bottle.

'I will help you pack,' said Fanny.

Sir Charles shrugged. 'The servants will do that.'

'I do not think so,' said Fanny gloomily. 'We are in disgrace with the mistress, so that means we are in disgrace with the servants, particularly servants who will have learned we have no money to give them. Servants who know there are no veils coming to them can be very bitter. So no arguments, Charles.' She led the way into his room.

He sat down on the bed and pulled off his boots while Fanny threw open the lid of one of his trunks. 'We have not tried this bed yet; Fanny,' he said.

She swung round, her eyes wide. 'Charles! How can you think of . . . you know . . . at this time of the day—and when we are both in such disgrace?'

He smiled lazily and held out his hand. 'T'would be very comforting, Fanny, to be disgraceful together. Besides, you need to get out of that gown anyway.'

She walked over to him. 'It will look most odd.'

186

He pulled her on top of him, caressed her breast, and said huskily, 'Who will see us?'

*   *   *

Several ladies of the ton were at that moment calling on Lady Denham to lay the latest piece of gossip at the feet of London's arch snob.

Lady Denham was gratifyingly appalled. To think she had actually entertained that precious pair in her home! It was no use, she said severely, everyone castigating poor Bohun for pulling a dagger on Deveney. The whole affair was enough to try the patience of a saint.

'I have heard,' said Mrs Bidford, 'that poor Amanda Woodward is quite heartbroken.

An unlovely light shone in Lady Denham's pale eyes. 'Well, that is no matter. She appeared to be *nutty* over my cousin, Raglin, last Season and *led him on* disgracefully—and then when he was about to drop the handkerchief, she started to flirt with Crumley, who is fifty if he's a day.'

'But rich,' pointed out Mrs Bidford caustically.

'I do not blame the Woodwards for concentrating on money,' announced Lady Denham. 'Marriages are not made in heaven, as we very well know. One must look to the future of one's homes and estates.'

And the loveless ladies clustered about her over the tea tray nodded wisely.

187

Lady Varney said, 'They will be cut everywhere. That goes without saying. And that poor creature, Martha Grimes, who is making a cake of herself over that army captain, will never raise her head again. The best thing she can do, the only decent thing to do, is to take herself off to foreign parts.'

'Foreign parts' for a lady was the equivalent of a pearl-handled revolver left discreetly on the study desk for a disgraced gentleman.

'One could forgive them for tricking La Woodward and that cur, Bohun. But to pretend to be wealthy!'

There was a murmur of approval. Mrs Bidford clenched her hands on her gown, for her gloves were a trifle worn—and in order to 'do' the Season and keep up a good front, it had been necessary to go in for many distressing and petty economies. She had a sudden flash of sympathy for the Deveneys.

'I might call on them,' she said airily.

'Who?' exclaimed Lady Varney. 'The Woodwards?'

'No, the Deveneys.'

'Why?' demanded Lady Denham awfully.

'They are at least interesting,' drawled Mrs Bidford, with fashionable languor. 'It is all really very amusing when you think of it. Besides, I am desperately curious to hear their excuses.'

'They will not receive you,' said a plump matron, Mrs Dark.

'Oh, I think they will,' said Mrs Bidford. 'I am sure the poor dears will be glad to see anyone.'

'As one of society's most fashionable leaders,' intoned Lady Denham, 'it is my place to call on them and tell them what I think of them.'

'Well, really,' said Mrs Bidford huffily, 'my reasons were to be kind.'

Lady Denham fixed her with a cold stare. 'They are not deserving of kindness. That would only make it look as if society were condoning their disgrace. No, I shall go. In fact'—she rose to her feet—'I shall go *now*.'

Lady Varney's eyes lit up with malicious amusement. 'My dear Lady Denham, not one of us here is going to let you face them alone. We will *all* go.'

*   *   *

'So much for packing,' said Fanny sleepily. 'I am going to be good. The sooner we are out of here, the better for Miss Grimes. No, do not try to stop me.' She collected her underwear from the floor beside the bed and put it on, then pulled on her crumpled gown. 'I will wash and change as soon as my conscience is easier, and it is not going to be easier until we are packed.'

The sun shone into the room and lit on a dusty brass-bound trunk in the corner. 'What is this?' asked Fanny, going over to it.

'Oh, that,' said Sir Charles. 'That's the Spanish woman's papers.'

Fanny gave the trunk a tug to try to move it toward the center of the room. 'It is very heavy.'

'It weighs a ton, my sweeting, and is no doubt full of ledgers every bit as brass-bound and locked as that trunk.'

'Can I see inside?'

'Why, my Pandora? Can you read Spanish?'

'No, but you said you could. It might be very interesting.'

'And stop us packing.'

'Just one peek.'

'Very well. I have the key somewhere.' He got out of bed and stretched his naked body.

'Hardly on your person,' said Fanny, with a giggle. 'Do put some clothes on. Where did you get that dreadful scar?'

'A saber cut at Corunna,' he said, pulling on his small clothes. 'Now, where did I put that key? Must you look inside now, Fanny?'

'Yes!'

He went to a trunk and fished inside, and at last produced an oilskin packet and carried it over to the bed and shook it out. Various objects fell on the bed cover: a tinderbox, several seals, a nail buffer, and a brass key.

'That is it. You are going to be very disappointed.'

He knelt down and fitted the key in the lock

190

and turned it. He threw back the lid. Across the top was a gold silk shawl embroidered with silk scarlet roses. It had a deep fringe. Fanny snatched it up. 'How beautiful!' she cried. She stood up, swung it about her shoulders, and did a pirouette.

'Fanny,' said Sir Charles in a hoarse whisper. 'Come here.'

She went to him and knelt down beside him.

They both stared into the trunk.

Myriads of jewels flashed up at them: the fiery prisms of diamonds, the slumbering blue of sapphires, green glow of emeralds, burning flame of rubies, and the heavy shine of gold, and more gold.

There was a folded piece of paper in one corner of the box. He opened it and read it.

Fanny found her voice. 'What does it say?'

'It says, "All my worldly goods I leave to Colonel, Sir Charles Deveney, with thanks to him for his bravery, courtesy, and kindness. I told him this contained only papers and family records in case his servants should learn of the worth and steal from him. I go to God. Elvira de Santos y Parva de Castille." And her signature is witnessed.'

Fanny said in a weak voice, 'Does this mean we are rich, Charles?'

'Very rich. Even after we build a monument to our gracious Spanish lady and light candles for her.'

'Oh, look, Charles. Look at this diamond-

and-sapphire comb.'

'Your curls are still too short to wear a Spanish comb.'

'Not a bit of it. I fit it here . . . like so.'

'Now you look like a princess you ought to be. Here is a diamond-and-sapphire necklace.' He clasped it about her neck. Fanny laughed and took out an emerald brooch and pinned it on her gown. He found a belt with a huge ruby clasp and she stood up and put it about her waist.

They seemed to have been overtaken by a temporary madness as he fished out more jewels, rings for every finger, bracelets for her arms, more necklaces about her neck, until she laughed and said, 'I am so weighted down with jewels, I can hardly move. Take something yourself!'

He fitted rings on his long, slim white fingers, and then, putting on his shirt and cravat and waistcoat, proceeded to star his cravat with jeweled stickpins and ornament his waistcoat with diamond studs.

'Now take my arm, Fanny,' he cried. 'We will go to Aunt Martha—and just you wait until you see the look on her face!'

*   *   *

Aunt Martha was looking bleakly at the faces of the visiting ladies, headed by Lady Denham. Those faces showed malice, avid curiosity, and spite. Only Mrs Bidford looked on her with anything approaching pity.

'We are come,' said Lady Denham, 'to tell Sir Charles and Lady Deveney what we think of their infamous behavior.'

Mrs Bidford clenched those soiled gloves again. She looked from Miss Grimes's haunted face to the faces of the other ladies. Suddenly she said, 'I only called, Miss Grimes, to see if there was anything I could do to help, and to tell you that you, and Captain Hawkes, and Sir Charles, *and* Lady Deveney can expect to receive a welcome from me at my home any time any of you care to call.'

The other ladies looked at her in horror.

'I don't care,' said Mrs Bidford almost tearfully, for she was wondering whether her husband would ever forgive her when he got to hear of her shameful behavior. 'Whom have they tricked? Greedy society. Whom have they shamed? Only one silly flirt who needed a lesson . . . and one ornament of the Fancy with the morals of a trull.'

Lady Denham gathered her shawl closely about her shoulders—as if a cold breath of unfashionable behavior should give her the ague. 'In all the years I have known you, Mrs Bidford, I have never seen you behave so badly. No one who wishes to be my friend will ever speak to the Deveneys again.'

'Good,' said Miss Grimes in a harsh voice. 'If no one wants to speak to either of the

Deveneys, you may take your leave . . . and as quickly as possible!'

The ladies, with the exception of Mrs Bidford, rose.

At that moment the double doors to the sitting room were flung open by a broadly beaming Hoskins—and all goggled at the glittering spectacle that stood on the threshold.

'Fanny! Charles! Where did you get those jewels?' screamed Miss Grimes.

Sir Charles's eyes ranged round the ladies' faces. 'Why, Aunt Martha,' he said. 'I am afraid we have been playing with my fortune like two children. What a spectacle we must look. But Fanny begs you to come with us and take your pick of whatever you want.'

Miss Grimes thought faintly that Charles had tricked some jeweler into lending them a fortune, but her loyalty lay with them and not these ladies of the ton. 'How very kind of you,' she said weakly. 'These ladies are on their way out. You must not receive them, for they are here to give you some tiresome jaw-me-dead, with the exception of Mrs Bidford, who stood out against them all with her offer of kindness.'

Fanny unclasped a glittering diamond brooch from her gown, ran to Mrs Bidford, and pressed it into that startled lady's hand, exclaiming, 'Take this trifle, although your offer of kindness is worth more than any gems.'

Lady Varney glared at Lady Denham. 'You

had no right, Lady Denham, to speak for all of us. Why, I was just on the point of offering the Deveneys the hospitality of *my* home!' The others pressed around Fanny, each shouting above the other with offers of friendship, while Fanny stood in the middle of them, laughing with surprise, a small and glittering figure.

*　　　*　　　*

After the visitors had been got rid of—with some difficulty—Captain Tommy arrived and listened to the chorus of voices telling him about the Spanish fortune. The servants were sent to carry in the trunk and they sat around it on the drawing-room floor, taking out jeweled items, one after the other, until it seemed as if the whole carpet was covered in a blaze of light.

'You can sell out now,' said Tommy, 'and buy a fine place in the country.'

'I will sell out eventually,' said Sir Charles, 'but only when this war is over.'

'Charles,' said Fanny in dismay. 'Of what good is all this wealth if we are going to be separated so soon?'

'Duty is a hard taskmaster, my love. Tommy knows what I mean.'

'Oh, well,' said Fanny on a sigh. 'We should bank all this. It won't be of much use to me in Spain.'

'You are not going to Spain,' said Sir

Charles firmly. 'Let that be an end of the matter.'

'No, we will not be parted,' said Fanny.

'I am going with Tommy,' put in Miss Grimes. 'I can take care of Fanny.'

In vain did Sir Charles argue and protest. Nothing would move Fanny from her purpose.

'And what of your parents?' asked Miss Grimes at last.

'I shall set up a trust for both families,' said Sir Charles, 'from which they will receive a quarterly income. They will, of course, be unable to live within it, but it should give us an excuse for keeping them at bay. And now, Fanny, we shall make sure that Tommy and Aunt Martha have a very fashionable wedding.'

*   *   *

Everyone who was anyone crowded into St. George's, Hanover Square, on the following week. The tale of Fanny handing over a valuable diamond brooch to Mrs Bidford had gone the rounds and everyone else was eagerly hoping that the Jewel Heiress, as Fanny was being called, would press some jewelry on *them*.

Miss Grimes was splendid in gold satin with some of the famous Deveney diamonds in her hair. Captain Tommy was an elegant figure for the first time in his life in Weston's tailoring, reputed to be the fastest suit of clothes ever produced. Fanny, in rich cream satin, was bridesmaid, while Sir Charles was best man. There was no question anymore of any of them being in disgrace. Wealth conquered all.

Fanny recited the wedding vows under her breath, remembering her own wedding. When Miss Grimes had finally changed her name to Mrs Tommy Hawkes and Fanny walked behind her down the aisle, she looked around at all the smiling faces and was suddenly glad they were leaving London. She did not have the new Mrs Hawkes's tolerance for the cynical vagaries of society.

Lord Bohun stood outside, behind one of the church pillars, a hat pulled down about his face, as the wedding party swept past him. Tricked and double-tricked, he thought savagely. If the Deveneys were rich, then what had been their game?

He had just been to his club and the members had turned their backs on him.

The silly crowd was cheering the married couple and throwing rose petals. And then as he looked across the road, he saw a face he recognized peering through the curtains of a closed carriage.

He shouldered his way roughly through the crowd until he reached that carriage. He rapped on the glass with his cane. The glass was let down and Miss Woodward's beautiful face looked at him.

'They are a wicked couple,' said Lord Bohun solemnly, 'and we have been sorely used.'

The carriage door swung open. Mrs Woodward leaned forward and said across her daughter, 'You are the only one who understands. We would be honored if you would join us for some refreshment.'

Lord Bohun ducked his head and climbed into the carriage. Life was not so bad after all.

*   *   *

That night, Fanny wriggled into a more comfortable position in her husband's arms. 'Something is troubling me,' she murmured.

'What?'

'Our newly married couple in the room just along the corridor.'

'So?'

'I cannot imagine your Aunt Martha doing anything like this.'

'What can I do to take your mind off it?' teased her husband. 'Something like this . . . and this?'

'Oh, yes, Charles. Do it again!'

We hope you have enjoyed this Large Print book. Other Chivers Press or G.K. Hall & Co. Large Print books are available at your library or directly from the publishers.

For more information about current and forthcoming titles, please call or write, without obligation, to:

Chivers Press Limited
Windsor Bridge Road
Bath BA2 3AX
England
Tel. (01225) 335336

OR

G.K. Hall & Co.
P.O. Box 159
Thorndike, Maine 04986
USA
Tel. (800) 223-2336

All our Large Print titles are designed for easy reading, and all our books are made to last.